"Rick," Laurie gasped, "what if this isn't love? What if it's a mistake?"

Rick threw back his head and laughed. "Here," he said, taking her hand and pressing it to his cheek. "See this face? There's no mistaking what I feel. And here," he added, pressing her hand against his chest, "feel this heart? I promise you, it's no mistake. This is real, Laurie, this is life, and love."

"But maybe it's lust!"

"Oh, Lord, you're wonderful!" His laughter rumbled into a growl in his throat. "*This* is lust!"

He lifted her in his arms, and tossed her onto the bed. In the same swift movement he was straddling her body, his lips nibbling at the hollow of her throat. He kissed her neck, and face and ears, quickly, playfully, his teasing mouth and words coaxing giggles from her as she wiggled away.

"That, Laurie O'Neill, is lust," he said, rocking back on his heels at the foot of the bed. "But darlin', what happens later . . . when you're ready . . . that's love. . . ."

Bantam Books by Adrienne Staff and Sally Goldenbaum
Ask your bookseller for the titles you have missed

WHAT'S A NICE GIRL . . . ?
  (*Loveswept #97*)

WHAT ARE *LOVESWEPT* ROMANCES?

They are stories of true romance and touching emotion. We believe
those two very important ingredients are constants in our highly sensual
and very believable stories in the *LOVESWEPT* line. Our goal is to give
you, the reader, stories of consistently high quality that may sometimes
make you laugh, sometimes make you cry, but are always fresh and
creative and contain many delightful surprises within their pages.

Most romance fans read an enormous number of books. Those they
truly love, they keep. Others may be traded with friends and soon
forgotten. We hope that each *LOVESWEPT* romance will be a
treasure—a "keeper." We will always try to publish

LOVE STORIES YOU'LL NEVER FORGET
BY AUTHORS YOU'LL ALWAYS REMEMBER

The Editors

Kathleen

LOVESWEPT® • 124

Adrienne Staff and Sally Goldenbaum
Banjo Man

BANTAM BOOKS
TORONTO • NEW YORK • LONDON • SYDNEY • AUCKLAND

BANJO MAN

A Bantam Book / January 1986

*LOVESWEPT® and the wave device are registered trademarks
of Bantam Books, Inc. Registered in U.S. Patent and
Trademark Office and elsewhere.*

ISBN 0-553-21741-0

Published simultaneously in the United States and Canada

---

*Bantam Books are published by Bantam Books, Inc. Its
trademark, consisting of the words "Bantam Books" and
the portrayal of a rooster, is Registered in U.S. Patent and
Trademark Office and in other countries. Marca Registrada.
Bantam Books, Inc., 666 Fifth Avenue, New York, New
York 10103.*

PRINTED IN THE UNITED STATES OF AMERICA

O   0 9 8 7 6 5 4 3 2 1

Prologue

The lengths of wooden flooring were lined up in stripes, a slice of dark oak, then a light one, in perfect parallel patterns.

Polished to an impeccable sheen, the floor's surface brightly reflected the steady swing of the black skirt moving slowly down the long hall toward the Mother Superior's office. The rhythmic click of a single pair of black shoes and the steady ticktock of the huge grandfather clock in the convent's parlor were the only sounds breaking the morning stillness.

Laurie O'Neill coughed softly. *There*, she thought, *at least I know I'm still alive.* Tiny flecks of dust danced in the slanted panels of light that fell out of the parlor doorways, and Laurie found herself strangely hypnotized by their movement. She shivered.

Everything was so quiet. An unearthly quiet. She took a deep breath and rested one hand over her heart to press it into calmness. But she couldn't—and hadn't been able to for a long time now. Her whole being resisted the peace here at the convent. It lay in heavy folds all around her, and yet she couldn't touch it or become part of it. Why? Was there something the matter with her? She had tried so hard, had done everything right. And yet she was still filled with an emptiness that defied explanation or reason. It was just there, right in the center of her, a cold, hollow void that ached to be filled.

Reaching the end of the hallway, Laurie paused and listened. In the distance she could just barely hear the beginnings of a chant. Matins. The sisters were all gathered in the high-ceilinged chapel for meditation and morning prayer. Listening intently to the lovely, pure sounds, Laurie gazed at the wide front hallway, lingering on the ornately carved front door.

In that instant she was swept back five years, to the crisp September morning when she and her best high-school friend, Ellen Farrell, had come through the same huge double doors, hearts thumping, hands shaking, their last cigarettes stubbed out with dramatic sighs and tossed into the bushes just outside the door. It had been five years since they'd thrown their heads back, their eyes bright with the naive dreams of youth, and begun the postulancy of the Sisters of Divine Mercy.

Ellen had lasted exactly six weeks. She'd been the class clown, the one who got them to laugh through those early, tense days when rules were carefully laid out as neatly as the boards in the floor and silence was wrapped around them in suffocating folds. Ellen had teased them all through it in her lighthearted, irreverent way, until the rules and regime seemed bearable, acceptable—a part of life. And then she left. It was early one morning, just like today.

She'd been asked not to tell anyone, and Laurie still remembered acutely the stabbing fear she'd felt that day in chapel when Ellen's place was empty. And then it was empty again at vespers. And Laurie knew her best friend in all the world had left. She'd cried into her pillow for many nights afterward, but finally was able to move ahead. After all, the postulancy mistress had pointed out, she hadn't joined the convent for Ellen. *She'd* be just fine. Ellen simply wasn't cut out for this kind of life; but she, Laurie O'Neill, had the true calling.

Laurie's gray eyes darkened with pain. *But no . . . she did not have it.* And now the silent hours and moments of her life here were drawing swiftly to a close.

It was time to go.

Squaring her shoulders, Laurie rounded the corner and entered the Mother Superior's office to sign the papers that would release her from her temporary vows.

Mother Joan Mary hugged her kindly and wished her well. But it was a shame, the Mother Superior added softly as she moved toward the door. Laurie had seemed happy as a sister, had seemed to be such a beautiful bride of the Church. "Yes, it is a real shame, Sister Loretta Ann," she whispered again as she slipped out the door and left Laurie alone to wipe away the tears and change into her clothes for whatever waited outside.

Well, Laurie thought stubbornly as she stepped out of the heavy black skirt and slid the veil off her head, perhaps it was a shame. But it was *right*. No matter what her family thought, when she'd explained it all on visiting day, no matter what the other sisters said, no matter how scared she was . . . deep down inside herself she had the solid comfort of knowing she, Laurie O'Neill, was right.

At the moment, that was little comfort indeed. Panic fluttered in her throat, the same panic that had kept her awake at night for weeks now, worrying and wondering about what lay ahead. How would she face the world she had left behind when she was eighteen? How would she handle it all? The prospect of even the simplest things, like eating alone in a restaurant, buying her own clothes, meeting people—meeting men!—froze her blood and made her heart thud painfully in her chest.

Her fingers fumbled at the snaps of her blouse. For just a second she wanted to cry, *I can't do it! I'm not brave enough!*, and give in to defeat. She'd stay, hiding her head beneath the crisp white convent sheets, and never come out. It was the thought of men that did it.

Would they be attracted to her? How would she react to them? Certainly not the way she had at eighteen, when she was shy and obedient to her parents' commands. And yet . . . and yet there was a yawning gulf created by five years in the convent that seemed suddenly impossible to cross. She had grown older, but certainly no wiser in relation to the opposite sex! What did she know about dating? Kissing? Touching? Loving!

Quickly she rubbed her eyes with her fingers, swallowed hard, and tipped up her chin. It was a delicate chin, but stubborn, part of the ingrained, time-honed Irish stubbornness that made her square her narrow shoulders, stiffen her spine, and fasten her even white teeth over her full, trembling lower lip. She'd come this far. She was not going to be beaten now.

She tore at the wrappings on the parcel-post package Ellen had sent, and only then did the ripples of fear begin to ease and make room for growing excitement about what lay ahead. In less than a day she'd be with Ellen—and beginning her new life!

Ellen had written not to worry, that she'd take care of everything; and she had, from the brown cotton dress to the handbag to the beat-up Mercury she'd arranged for Laurie to drive to D.C. Laurie grinned. Ellen might be a bit crazy, but she was certainly the best friend a girl could have.

"You must come home first," her father had insisted when she'd told him of her plans. But that was the one thing Laurie O'Neill knew with all her heart she couldn't do. Not yet. If she fell back into the protective embrace of her family now, before she had her feet firmly planted on the ground, she might never be able to stand alone.

With renewed determination Laurie pulled the dress over her head and glanced hastily into a glass-fronted cabinet. A long, needle-sharp shiver raced through her whole body, from head to toe. So much of her showed! A goodly portion of leg, all of each arm, and, above the gently scalloped neckline, the pale, translucent skin of her chest and neck. She felt naked! Grabbing a long-sleeved sweater Ellen had mercifully thrown in, she dared a second glance into the cabinet.

How would others see her? she wondered. Was she pretty? Would people on the outside like her? She tried a smile, and pushed her fingers nervously through her clipped coppery hair. Would she meet men? How? And if she did, what in heaven's name would she have to talk about—the merits of wearing a serge habit in the dead of winter?

"Laurie O'Neill," she scolded aloud, "you've put the cart way before the horse! Cut the melodrama and get going!"

Slipping her stockinged feet into a pair of beige flats, she smoothed the dress and snapped open the pocketbook. Ellen had thought of everything—

lipstick, blusher, a wallet for the money her parents had sent, a little map directing her to Ellen's apartment in Washington, a tiny, airplane-sized bottle of Irish whiskey, with a note—"for medicinal purposes"—taped on the side, and a small handkerchief. Ellen had folded a tiny piece of paper into the cloth, and Laurie read it slowly: *Wrap up your tears in this, and leave them there in Pennsylvania. The sun's in the sky, God's in His heaven, and I'm here in Washington waiting for you. All's right with the world, and it awaits you, Laurie O'Neill!*

The world awaits you . . . "And I'm ready for you," Laurie breathed softly. "I hope . . ."

With one long, sweeping glance she committed to memory the place that had been home for five years, then slipped silently out into the blustery February morning and began the long drive to Washington, D.C., to Ellen's apartment, to a new job . . . and her brand-new life.

One

Laurie brushed the damp tendrils of hair off her forehead and tried to force some life back into her exhausted body. Dropping the drab brown suitcase to the floor outside Ellen's apartment, she looked dimly at her wristwatch: 3:02 A.M.

And she hadn't even had the presence of mind to *call* Ellen. Not when her brakes failed, not when she took the wrong exit. Not when she pulled over to the side of the road to wipe the tears away. Ellen wouldn't be expecting her anymore, would think she was coming in the next day. Ellen would suppose . . . but Laurie couldn't think anymore.

She knocked weakly on the door.

The soft, dim light in the silent hallway cast eerie shadows around her, and she knocked again, shifting from one foot to the other. She had lived an eternity in one day, and she was ready for it to come to an end! Shattering the night stillness, she pounded more loudly on the door, and the sound bounced off the thinly papered walls.

The shuffling behind the closed door had barely

reached her ears when the lock clicked and the door was flung open.

Laurie's mouth dropped open, but no words came out. Facing her, with but inches between his bare chest and her trembling self, was an incredibly handsome, very sleepy-looking man, lazily tugging up the zipper on his faded jeans.

If she were ever going to faint, now was the time to do it. How nice simply to pitch over onto her face and wake up to find Ellen standing there, instead of . . . instead of this unimaginably gorgeous half-naked man. *Come on, knees,* she prayed, *do your thing.*

But nothing happened.

Of course not, a tiny voice inside her mocked. How can you faint when you're so busy staring at his chest? But there was nothing on it! And it was right there in front of her, such an amazingly virile chest, the skin dark and smooth, dusted with dark, curly hair. And there were so many muscles: the sculpted curve of muscle across his upper chest, the flat, hard band of muscle flowing down between his ribs to his navel, and then the lean muscular patch of belly visible inside the zipper's open V. Oh, Lord . . . what in the world was she doing?

Laurie's eyes flew to his face and met a sleepy, amused grin. "Well, that was quite a once-over, ma'am," he drawled. "Do I get my turn now?" He winked and tugged his zipper higher, buttoned his jeans, and settled them comfortably low on his lean hips. His eyes never left Laurie's face.

Every nerve in Laurie's body seemed to flame. Her head began to spin, and black spots as big as whales swam before her eyes. Well, she thought resignedly, better late than never. And as her eyes clung to the fading image of the man in front of her, her knees gave way.

The stranger caught her to him, and held her tightly there, pressed against his sleep-warmed body. "Hey, hold on. Are you okay? Hey—" He curved one arm around her back to hold her slender weight, then used his free hand to brush the damp, clinging strands of hair off her pale cheeks. "I was only teasing. My bark is definitely worse than my bite!"

He stared down at the trembling girl in his arms, and a strange tightness closed his throat. She was lovely, with a beauty as fragile and haunting as the heroines in the old ballads he loved. Cursing himself silently, he tipped up her chin and drew a hand gently across her brow. When he spoke aloud, his voice held a husky gentleness. "Hey, there, I'm sorry, sweet thing; I didn't mean to frighten you. I'm no dangerous sex fiend, just a half-awake banjo player with a rough sense of humor."

Laurie heard the words from far away, as if she were floating somewhere high overhead, or deep beneath the waves. She tried to answer, to assure him that she was absolutely fine and didn't mean to be so silly, but she couldn't quite find her voice. Her lashes fluttered open, revealing huge gray eyes filled with dismay and embarrassment, and her gaze brushed his face like a butterfly's wing.

Rick Westin felt the touch of that gaze, and reacted to it instantly. In one strong sweep he had Laurie up in his arms, cradled against his chest. He pushed the door open all the way with one hip, and strode into the room. For a moment he hesitated in front of the sofa, but shook his head and went right through the living room and into the only bedroom.

The blankets were thrown back, the sheets wrinkled from his weight. The pillow still bore the imprint of his head. Without a word he bent, placed Laurie on the bed, and sat down on the edge next to her, his jean-clad thigh agonizingly close to Laurie's bare arm.

Squeezing her eyes closed, she crossed both arms over her breasts, her hands clenched into small, shaky fists.

Rick laughed. "You look like you're ready to give up the ghost, darlin'. Relax. You're safe here, I promise." But there was a husky sensuality in his voice that made him sound anything but safe. "Relax," he ordered again, prying her hands loose and running his palms slowly down her arms in what was meant to be a comforting gesture.

Little did he know the effect he was having on Laurie O'Neill.

"I—I don't think I can relax like this," she said with a gasp, struggling toward the far end of the bed. "Maybe if you went away . . . or if *I* got up and went away . . . or something."

"Then you're feeling a little better?"

"No, I don't think so. I can't breathe, and . . . and my heart's pounding."

"I know. I can feel it."

"Ohhhh," Laurie groaned, not wanting to be reminded of just how close their bodies were. "Let me go. I think I can stand up now."

"Sure?"

"No! I'm not sure about *anything,* except that I'm tired and miserable, and I must be lost—"

"Why?"

"Because you couldn't possibly be sleeping here if this is where *I'm* supposed to be staying. Ellen wouldn't do that to me. She couldn't! She'd have warned me—" Laurie wailed.

"Whoa! So you're Ellen's long-lost friend! Listen, she figured you'd changed your mind, when you didn't call. So she let me con her into staying overnight. You see"—he rambled on, seeking to soothe her with the steady, comforting timbre of his voice—"I found this great mutt of a dog on the road last Sunday and brought him home, and now I'm having my place bombed for fleas. The dog's at the vet's, being similarly treated, and I needed a place to stay tonight. Ellen had graveyard duty in the Emergency Room, and you weren't here, so everything worked out fine. Or was *supposed* to, anyway. There." He stopped talking and pushed her gently back against the pillow. "Now you know you're not lost. What can I do about tired and miserable, hmmm?"

When he smiled, Laurie felt shivers dance up her arms. Before she had only been aware of his body, that surprising, shocking seminakedness, the darkly tanned flesh. Now, as if for the first time, she saw his face. He had rather wild dark hair, a lot of it, and very dark eyes, a strong, sensual mouth, and a sharp cleft in his chin, half hidden by the heavy shadow of beard that darkened his jaw. But it was his eyes that hypnotized her; they were a brown so dark and warm it needed another name. Cocoa, she mused, or chocolate, or coffee.

Nervous laughter bubbled in her throat. "I must be hungry." She gasped, struggling to get hold of herself. That had to be the explanation: hunger and exhaustion, and shock! What else could explain these crazy thoughts and feelings that were tumbling around inside her?

The banjo player, studying her with those piercing dark eyes, accepted her words as answer to his question. "Well, sweet thing, I can take care of that! A Westin special, coming up!"

He brushed his fingers lightly across her cheek, rose to his full, lanky height, and headed for the kitchen. At the doorway, he turned to Laurie. "You stay there, now. No funny business. I don't want to come back and find you fainted dead away on the floor."

"Really, you don't have to worry about me, or fuss over me, or anything," she whispered, pushing herself up onto her elbows. "I'm okay. And just a cup of tea or a glass of milk would be fine. Don't go to any bother, please."

"I don't know," he answered softly, "but I think I'd like bothering over you. You remind me of some little bird that's been blown about on the wind and needs a place to rest."

"I am not!" she retorted, startling herself with her uncharacteristic burst of anger. Swinging her legs over the side of the bed, she glared at him, her gray eyes wide and flashing. "I'm not a little bird. No, not at all. I'm a grown woman, out on my own, and I can take care of myself. If I can drive from western Pennsylvania to Washington, D.C., without brakes, I can do anything. And I intend to. And I don't want to be mothered or smothered or . . . or—"

"Whoa!" His rich laughter filled the room. "Fantastic. You can bet I won't make that mistake again. And believe me, mothering and smothering were not what I had in mind. I've just got a feeling that tonight might be the luckiest night of my life. I owe Ellen a kiss and Arlo an extra scratch behind the ears. Now, you just sit still, and I'm gonna fix you one of my special midnight snacks. Well"—he chuckled, glancing at the clock—"make that a three A.M. special, comin' up for . . . Hey! you know, I don't even know your name."

"I'm probably better off that way!" Laurie tossed back, a tiny smile tugging at the corner of her mouth totally against her will. "My name is Laurie O'Neill. Pleased to meet you. And you are . . . ?"

". . . even more pleased to meet you!" Flashing a rather wolfish grin, he moved swiftly from the doorway to her side. He captured her hand between the two of his.

Messages sparked up the nerves of her arm, warning her startled brain about the deceptive strength of his hands and the surprisingly sensual rasp of the callused pads of his fingertips against her palm. His touch was cool, but her entire arm blazed with hidden warmth. She pulled her hand away as though she'd been burned. "No, I meant your name," she insisted with ill-restrained exasperation. "Is Westin your first, last, or only?"

"Ah . . . an old-fashioned girl who likes formal introductions. Well"—he offered her his hand and a wry grin—"I'm Rick Westin. Banjo player, balladeer, and collector of all kinds of American bits and pieces: songs, stories, people, and places. Satisfied?"

Laurie tucked both hands warily behind her back. "Yes . . . mostly."

Hunkering down at the side of the bed, he rested his palms on his denim-clad thighs and lifted one dark brow in question. "All right. What else do you want to know?"

"Well, it's probably none of my business. . . ."

"Come on. Shoot."

"How . . . how do you know Ellen?"

"You mean how? Or how well?" he asked bluntly.

Laurie went from pale to sheet-white. "I meant *how!* I'd never pry, or ask anything like that!"

"Why not? Everyone else would." He narrowed his dark eyes and looked at her for a long moment. Then he added with calculated sarcasm, "I mean . . . you did find me in her bed."

"Stop it! I didn't think . . . think anything of it even for a moment. And I'd never make insinuations like that anyway; it's none of my business. Ellen is a good friend, and I care about her. As long as she's happy, well, that's all that matters."

Rick thought for a second that she was putting

him on, but no, nobody was that good an actress. This kid was sincere.

"Sorry." He grinned, too pleased with his discovery to sound totally repentant. "You know, that's nice, really nice. I told you this was my lucky night! Now I'm gonna get you that invigorating, rejuvenating one-hundred-percent-natural, high-energy, low-calorie, mid-octave whippersnapper of a Westin special. Stay where you are!"

He left Laurie seesawing silently between anger and amazement.

When he had disappeared safely into the kitchen, and could be heard clanking noisily through cabinets and drawers, Laurie dropped back onto the pillow in exhaustion. She lay still for a moment, her arms limp at her sides, her hands curled on the sheet like pink shells on white sand.

Slowly, she became aware of a disturbingly earthy, intoxicating scent. Furrowing her brow, she breathed in deeply, letting the smell fill her head and lungs. With surprise she realized it hadn't drifted in from the kitchen, as she had assumed, but rose around her from the bed and pillow where she lay. It was vaguely familiar, but alien, too, and elusively avoided every label she tried to pin on it.

She closed her eyes, and drew another heady breath . . . and suddenly an image flashed on the dark screen of her closed lids: It was herself, so young—sixteen, maybe, or seventeen—curled half-asleep in bed, her own bed in her own bedroom back in the big white frame house in Pittsburgh, the bed with the canopy, and the faded roses climbing the wallpaper . . . and she was hugging something in her arms, something redolent of that same musky, arousing scent. Catching her lower lip between her teeth, Laurie concentrated on the memory, willing it into focus.

And there it was. She was hugging a sweater! Some boy's letter sweater, white wool with a navy band at hem and cuff, and a big, proud B for the Bulldogs. The scent that filled her head then, and now, was a male smell, of after-shave and sweat and that secret, undeniably foreign and exciting scent of . . . sex!

Laurie leaped upright in bed, her body damp with the cold sweat of fear. For she remembered well what had happened next: her father's footsteps in the hall and the bright glare of light, and his anger as he pulled the sweater away and crushed it in his hands. "That is all right for your sister; Katy doesn't have your potential, Laurie, so she might as well waste herself on being boy-crazy. But not you! You are my gift, my brightest daughter. And I'm ashamed of you. *You* must save yourself for greater things."

That was all.

The sweater was hanging on a hook by the front door the next morning, and Laurie picked it up and took it back to the boy at school without a word of explanation. Joe, that was his name, Joe Holzpath. A nice boy . . . And when she graduated, she left home and joined the convent, and her father and mother and all the aunts were so very proud.

Tears filled her eyes and spilled suddenly down Laurie's cheeks. Wrapping her arms around her knees, she buried her face against her skirt and cried as she had not cried since that night years before. Her narrow shoulders shook with sobs, and her chest ached with their stifled force. Oh, what had happened to her life? All those days and years gone. But not wasted, oh, please, *no.* She had tried, she had been a good person, a good teacher, there was certainly meaning to it all, to what rested in the past. Please, let there be some meaning to what was waiting ahead!

The sudden whir of the blender in the kitchen startled her back to the present. Wiping her face on the blanket, she stood up and tiptoed into the bathroom.

The girl who stared back at her from the mirror over the sink looked desperately in need of restoration. Her inexpertly cut hair was badly tangled and her skin was far too pale. Laurie splashed cold water on her face, borrowed a brush from the cabinet, and pinched some color into her cheeks. Then she practiced a smile. And when she was satisfied that it would stay where it was supposed to, and not quiver into a frown, she straightened her shoulders, tipped up her chin, and headed for Rick Westin and his red-eye special.

She only made it as far as the living room when she tripped over something big, black, and hard in the dark.

"Ow!" she yelped, cradling her stubbed toe in one hand.

Rick sauntered in, flipped on the light, and shook his head. "And you said you drove all the way from Pennsylvania by yourself?" There was a distinct note of disbelief in his voice.

"Yes. Yes, I certainly did. And without brakes."

"Sounds like a fool thing to do, woman. I'm all for a little risk, but even *I* wouldn't try such a drive."

Laurie scowled at him and dropped onto the sofa. She sighed dramatically and rolled her eyes. "Listen, I didn't plan it that way! I'm really a very calm, sensible, practical person."

"Sure."

"Yes, I am! It so happens that I had just gotten out . . . out of my hometown, and headed across the mountains, and I lost my brakes. Ellen's brother delivered the car, and said he had checked it out, so I thought everything was fine. It wasn't—" She stared him down, daring him to challenge her story, then shrugged lightly and added, "So I did what I had to do. I drove here. And here I am. And what in the world are all these cases and why are they lying around in the dark?"

"Banjos."

"Banjos? All of them?"

"Yup! Mostly five-string, some a hundred years old, some all the way from Possum Hollow, Kentucky." His dark eyes shone with a glint of pure, joyous delight. "Look at that one," he said, pointing to a dark shape in the corner. "It's so purty, I wish I could play the case!"

His enthusiasm was as contagious as measles, and Laurie grinned. "I've never heard anyone talk that way about a banjo before."

"No, guess not." He laughed softly, averting his face. Then he met her eyes, and held them with his dark, intense gaze. "Someday I'm going to love a woman the way I love these banjos, and we'll make our own kind of music together. Then I won't have to ride to the moon alone."

Laurie's eyes were round as saucers. Why was he telling her this? What did he mean?

But before she could ask, Rick leaped to his feet, avoiding her eyes now, and strode to the kitchen. In a second he was back with a tall glass of some frothy amber liquid and a small plate of coarse dark bread spread with honey. "Here, get yourself some energy, sweet thing."

"Would you *please* stop calling me that!" Laurie demanded, her hand poised in midair.

"Why? It suits you."

"How do you know? You don't know a thing about me."

"But I bet I'm right! Wanna bet? And let me see, now, what would be an appropriate prize?"

"You're crazy!" She laughed, accepting the glass from his hand and taking a tiny sip. "Ummm—this is wonderful. What is it?"

"A banana–yogurt–summer-squash shake."

"Ugh!" Laurie held the glass at arm's length and stared at it. "Are you kidding?"

"Nope." He laughed, that now-familiar glint flashing in his dark eyes. "Go on, drink it down. Guaranteed by Aunt Jess Winters in Skytop, Tennessee, to cure what ails you. Whatever it may be!"

"And the bread . . . first tell me what's in it!"

"Rye, rolled oats, whole wheat and wheat germ, sorghum molasses. I made it myself."

"You're not serious!"

"Anyone ever tell you you've got a real skeptical side to your nature?"

"No one's ever fed me health food in the middle of the night before," Laurie retorted, smiling.

"Their loss, my gain," Rick answered, a teasing grin tugging at one corner of his mouth. Then he rose, picked up a banjo case, and came back to sit next to Laurie on the sofa, his thigh stretched intimately alongside hers.

She felt the heat of his body through their clothes and stiffened. Forbidding her hands to tremble or her voice to quake, she quipped with feigned nonchalance, "I bet that banjo has a story to tell."

Rick pinned her with a glance that saw right through her masquerade, but his dark eyes were as gentle as they were penetrating. He studied Laurie briefly, then bent his head and concentrated on the banjo case in his hands. "This banjo, here, was made before the Civil War. I got it from a man who got it from a man who got it from the great Doc Hopkins. That makes me one lucky fellow."

Tossing her a boyish grin, he snapped open the case and withdrew the long-necked instrument. "You asked how I met Ellen? Well, it all started with this banjo. When I got it, some of the parquet work here on the neck was chipping. It was late one night after a show, and I was dog-tired and ready to drop, but when my manager handed me this baby, well, I just had to get to work on her. Went to cut a spare piece of wood and slashed my arm open. Ellen was on duty that night in Emergency. Like tonight."

"Oh, how terrible!"

"Sure was. I bled all over the drumhead, and had to replace it. Damn!"

Laurie shook her head in disbelief. "No, I meant *you*. It must have hurt."

"I'm tough," he answered simply, a grin spreading over his handsome face. "But I never object to a little sympathy and comfort, especially from a beautiful woman—"

Laurie was on her feet and talking before he could finish his sentence. "You know, I think what I really need is a little sleep. I'm supposed to start work tomorrow, and—"

"That's all right. I've got early rehearsals. Just leave the stuff; I'll clean up. You take the bedroom and I'll toss my body on the couch."

"Oh, no, I wouldn't hear of it!" How could she ever explain to him about the bed? There was no way she could sleep on that pillow, that sheet. "No! I insist that I take the couch! It's only fair."

Rick forked one hand through his tousled hair, then crossed his arms solidly over his chest and dropped onto the couch. "You want to argue about this, sweet thing? Or you want to get some rest?"

"I . . . guess I'll get some rest," Laurie whispered, edging backward toward the bedroom.

"Good. Sleep tight."

Nodding pleasantly, she slipped through the door, shut it behind her and collapsed against it, her strength pouring out through the soles of her feet like water from a sieve. So much for any hope of sleep tonight!

Through the wall, she heard Rick moving about in the other rooms. Then the bright slice of light beneath the door vanished, and all was quiet.

Quiet as a mouse herself, Laurie slipped to the side of the bed and lay down, fully dressed, eyes staring at the ceiling. The minutes ticked by, slowly, bringing no easing of her tension. She felt like an overstretched banjo string, thrumming with the beat of her own pulse, ready to snap at a touch.

Sitting up, she partially loosened her dress, unfastened the belt, and lay down again. Then she was up, kicking off her shoes, peeling off her stockings. Lying down, she thought she was going to suffocate; she was afraid to breathe too deeply, afraid to close her eyes. She jumped up, slipped her dress off over her head, and tiptoed to the window in her prim white slip. Opening the window, she drew a steadying breath, then roamed silently about the room, pacing, counting her steps, and trying not to think—about anything!

I knew it, she grumbled softly to herself. *I should have had that glass of warm milk and never talked to him! I should have stopped and called Ellen, as I said I would. I never should have left the convent on a weekend. Maybe . . . maybe, I never should have left at all.*

Covering her face with her trembling hands, she leaned against the wall. *Oh, I don't mean that, I really don't! I'm just scared, that's all, a little scared. Anyone would be, right? I've spent every long night for years in a tiny cell, with dozens of other women beyond the curtain. And tonight*

*who's there but a tall, sexy man with a bare chest
and warm, earth-brown eyes. Oh, I'm beginning
to sound like my sister Katy, or Ellen, or . . .*

Her wide gray eyes lit with laughter, which she
smothered quickly behind one hand. *Goodness,
I'm beginning not to sound like a nun! Now, that
may be a cause for celebration—one warm milk
coming up!*

Laurie stole to the door, pried it open silently,
and sneaked out into the living room. There she
stopped dead in her tracks.

Moonlight was pouring through the open
window, lighting the form on the couch with a
pale, golden glow. Rick Westin had one arm
thrown across his eyes, the other angled across his
bronzed chest. His bare legs were stretched the
length of the couch, his feet dangling over its arm.
Laurie's hand flew to her mouth. Now she knew
why they called them briefs! Not much of this man
was hidden, and both what she saw and what she
could imagine left her breathless.

Thank heavens he was sleeping!

Laurie leaned just a tiny bit closer, marveling at
the dark dusting of hair on his chest and thighs,
the golden glow of his skin, the loose power in his
limbs. And then she pinched herself, gulped a
huge breath of air, and spun back toward the
safety of her door.

But not in time.

Rick's soft, teasing "'Night, sweet thing!" caught
her. Pierced her like an arrow.

And when she finally managed to slip into the
less-wrinkled side of the bed and pressed her heavy
eyelids shut, the voice remained with her,
accompanied by the soft distant strains of a banjo.

Two

"Good morning, Paula," Laurie called to the secretary who was sitting just inside the suite of offices that housed Senator Murphy's ambitious staff.

"Well, and a good morning to you, Laurie!" The trim, gray-haired woman's face lit in a smile at the sight of the newest member of the staff. "You're looking mighty chipper this morning! Seems we haven't scared you off after your first week of work."

"Not by a long shot!" Laurie quipped. "To tell the truth, Paula, I love being busy. I love the bustle and chatter and responsibility—all the people I've met, and the feeling that I'm right at the heart of things."

Paula took off her glasses and rubbed the lenses absentmindedly with the edge of her sweater. "Yes, I know just what you mean. After my husband died, I knew I had better get out and get a job, or I'd end up sitting alone and stewing in my own misery. And the pace here does keep one's mind from dwelling on other things."

Laurie's mind was immediately filled with visions of high convent walls, and silent halls, and—

With a start, she realized that was not the only image she had been holding at bay all week. Conjuring up a totally opposite emotion was the sharp, tantalizing image of a lean, dark banjo player. Excitement quickened her blood.

Laurie blushed. Then, feigning nonchalance, she looked around the office. "Well, what does the good senator have in store for me today?"

"Plenty!" the older woman answered briskly, her tone effortlessly becoming businesslike as she handed Laurie a stack of notebooks. "The senator wants these facts researched before he goes back to Pennsylvania tomorrow. All the info's here. 'All you have to do is do it!' " She grinned as she repeated the jovial legislator's often-used dictum.

Laurie looked down at the papers, then back up at Paula. "But where?"

"Library of Congress. Thataway." She pointed out the window. "Just go out the east entrance, up South Capitol Street, and turn right on Independence. And if it's your first visit, you're in for a treat!" With that, she bowed her head over a pile of memos stacked precariously atop her desk.

Hugging the files to her chest, Laurie spun on her heel and marched briskly back out the door. Each day there were new things, unexpected, unpredictable things, to deal with: contact with public figures she had always relegated to another world, press conferences, cocktail parties, a pass by a coworker! And each day she felt more ready to handle them and less "different" than she had the day before. It was a wonderful feeling, one that warmed her heart and pushed away the fear she'd lived with these past months.

And much of this new confidence she owed to Ellen.

Dear Ellen, who had stumbled into her apartment at seven last Monday morning, yelped in surprise, and smothered Laurie in genuine affection. First she had handed over a battered suitcase full of outdated clothes sent ahead by Laurie's mother, and a half dozen phone messages from her father, and then she'd offered another hug of welcome. "Oh, I am *so* glad you're here, Laurie!"

They had perched on kitchen stools, their mugs of hot tea steaming on the counter top, as Ellen groaned and gasped her way through Laurie's retelling of her departure, perilous drive, and late-night arrival at the apartment.

"That brother of mine! I'll strangle him the next time I see him. Not checking the brakes! Where is that boy's good sense?"

"Oh, Ellen, don't scold! 'All's well that ends well.' "

"You call that 'ending well'? Getting here in the wee hours of the morning and finding Westin asleep in the bed? Hmm. I guess you *could* call that 'ending well,' though I'm surprised you're so . . . liberated!"

"Ellen!"

"Oh, I'm just teasing. But I bet you *were* surprised!"

"That's putting it mildly." Laurie giggled. "Remember the time we walked past the boys' locker room, just as they threw Steve Lanski out in his shorts? Well, I think I had the same expression on my face."

"Hysteria! Oh, my poor, innocent girl. You make me feel eighteen again, and that hasn't happened in quite a while. Laurie, tell me," Ellen prompted, her eyes warm with friendship, "are *you* still eighteen?"

Laurie hesitated for just a brief moment, then answered clearly and honestly. "I'm afraid so. In some ways, at least."

"Well! Then I'd better do a little protecting here. Westin, up and out!"

Disappearing faster than a rabbit in a magician's hat, she vanished into the living room, where she routed Rick Westin from his berth on the sofa. "Time to go home, handsome. Here are your pants. Your banjos. Your shirt. Call me later in the week and I'll cook you some dinner."

"Will that sweet thing be here?" he asked sleepily, pulling on his boots.

"Depends on how safe she'll be in your presence."

"Hey, you know me," he replied, managing to sound terribly wounded by her unjust accusation.

"That's exactly what I mean!" Ellen insisted, and their mingled laughter floated back to Laurie's hiding place in the kitchen.

She vowed to stay right there, unseen, but Rick's husky voice lured her out. "After all the trouble you put me through last night, Ms. O'Neill, don't I even get a good-bye?"

"Good-bye," she answered, stepping through the doorway.

"Good *morning.*" He grinned, stuffing his shirttail into the back of his jeans. "Sleep okay?"

"Fine, thank you," Laurie lied, heat suffusing her cheeks.

Ellen looked from one to the other with amused affection. "Well, I'll be . . . but that's enough chit-chat. Westin, out! This girl's got enough to face this morning without resisting your sex appeal to boot! 'Say good-bye, Gracie.' "

And with a grin he was gone, taking the banjos and the brightness of the morning with him.

But the nameless yearning he had awoken in

Laurie lingered on all week. Of course, it was only one facet of the confusion that kept her heart beating fast. There were others: her job, the newness of the city, the rush of strangers around her. It was all frightening . . . and wildly intoxicating.

Even now, her gray eyes blazed with delight as she headed up South Capitol Street and turned right on Independence. Here she was, Laurie O'Neill, just out of the convent, on her way to do research for a United States senator! Yes, all was right with the world.

Three hours later, a dozen sheets of notes tucked securely under her arm, Laurie walked briskly out of the Library of Congress and back to the Rayburn Building. Another job well done, Laurie O'Neill! she silently praised herself. See, you can do it! She quickened her step, broadened her smile, and rushed through the glass door to Senator Murphy's office.

"Hi, Paula! I—"

The words died in her throat. Leaning against the brass coatrack in the corner was a battered banjo case. And leaning on the edge of Paula's desk, his broad shoulders outlined by the soft flannel of his work shirt, was Rick Westin.

He spun toward her, his eyes lighting with pleasure. "Finally! Hello, sweet thing."

Happiness welled in Laurie's chest, as unexpected as spring rain in a drought. "Hi, yourself." She grinned. Then she caught Paula's amused glance and felt the heat climb above the collar of her blouse. "Paula, Rick . . . I guess you two have already met."

"We've had a delightful hour, Laurie," Paula assured her. "Rick was telling me about his travels through the Appalachians, and I was sharing a story I had heard years ago in Kentucky.

"Darnedest thing I ever knew. Goat wandered

into a wedding party and ate the dresses off all the bridesmaids, but didn't even nibble on the bride. Ate the groom's trousers, though, 'cept for the zipper!"

Laurie laughed. "Oh, you two! And here I've been slaving away all morning over these files. Unfair!"

Rick's response was sure and deliberate. "Let me make it up to you, darlin'," he said, taking the files from her arms and dropping them in a basket on Paula's desk. He curved one arm around her slender shoulders and turned her toward the door. "I'm taking you to lunch."

Laurie glanced quickly over her shoulder, uncertainty clouding her gray eyes. "But work . . . the senator . . ."

"Go on, Laurie," Paula urged her. "It's noon. Enjoy yourself."

"But—"

"Go on, child. That's a nice fellow you've got there." And without another word she returned to her work.

As they made their way down the hall, Laurie hesitantly fell into step beside Rick. What exactly had Paula meant? Rick Westin, with his wonderful eyes and wild, dark hair, was certainly not *Laurie's* fellow! Heavens, she wouldn't know what to do with a fellow, let alone this particular one! He'd cut through her naivete like a hot knife through butter. Just the thought made shivers dance up her spine.

Overcome with awkwardness, she glanced up at his face, and then quickly away. "I'm not sure you should have come to the senator's office, Rick. I mean, somehow it doesn't seem proper."

"Proper, heck! I would have tracked you down at the White House, Ms. O'Neill, if that was where you had happened to be! Couldn't stay away any longer."

The fire went racing through her blood again. Silently Laurie cursed her lack of control and prayed for a cool flippancy to match his. It seemed light-years beyond her grasp. How did they handle this kind of thing in the movies? No, that was no help at all. The last movie she had seen was *The Sound of Music*!

Beside her, Rick slung the banjo across his back and tightened his hold on Laurie's shoulder. He'd had this lovely coppery-haired lass on his mind for nearly five days now, and he wasn't about to let her get away until he figured out what to do about it.

"Aren't you just the littlest bit glad to see me?" he asked, smiling down at her.

"Yes, of course, Rick. It was a very pleasant surprise," she gulped out, trying to maintain some semblance of calm.

Every nerve in her body was aware of the unfamiliar weight of a man's arm across her shoulders, the solid feel of his muscle and bone, his latent power. His shirt sleeve tickled the nape of her neck. His hip brushed against hers with every stride. She was electrified with sensation.

Rick was unaware of the turmoil he was causing. "Well, what're you in the mood for, Laurie?" he asked.

"An aspirin . . . and an hour to catch my breath, Banjo Man," she quipped.

Rick's laugh was rich with surprise. "You are something else, darlin'! I have a feeling it's going to take me a good long time to figure you out."

"No," she insisted, shaking her head firmly. "There's not that much to figure out. Honest."

"Thou dost protest too much, methinks." He laughed, enjoying the slender warmth of her body within the curve of his arm. "Tell me about you, Laurie. Where you come from, who you are, how you like Washington and your job . . ."

Laurie picked the easiest—and safest—of the three. "Oh, I'm really enjoying Washington, Rick. It's such a beautiful city, and so exciting. And this job with Senator Murphy is just great!"

"I'd say! Were you on his staff back in Pennsylvania?"

"In . . . in Pennsylvania?" she stuttered. Slipping away from the confines of his arm, she stuffed her hands deep in her skirt pockets and stared at the floor. "Back in Pennsylvania I was a . . . teacher. Grade school. Kids. In Pittsburgh."

"Ah, a noble profession. I bet you were terrific."

"I was fine," she replied with a little shrug. "Very serious, very conscientious. Sometimes I thought the children taught me more than I was teaching them."

"Like what?" he asked softly.

"Oh . . . how to laugh, and be open to the experiences around them."

He nodded gravely. "I know what you mean. Not so many walls between them and life, for good or bad."

"Yes." Her wide gray eyes flew to his face. "Yes, not so many walls . . ."

He waited for a moment, thinking she was going to say more, but she didn't.

"So what made you leave?"

"I just needed to get away," Laurie whispered.

Rick slipped an arm around her waist and flashed a wide, sexy grin. "Well, I'm sure glad you got away to *here!*" And without any warning he bent his dark head and brushed his lips against the curve of her cheek, his breath stirring the curling tendrils of her hair and tickling her ear.

Laurie sucked in breath like a fish out of water.

"Rick, no! Are you crazy? This is a public building. Senators have their offices here!"

"Might as well start at the top!"

"Rich Westin!"

"Okay"—he laughed, feigning contrition—"I'll behave. For here and now. I promise."

"You had better," she flung back, her eyes and mouth round with surprise.

Still laughing, he cupped her elbow lightly in his large hand and led her out into the sunlight.

They walked up Independence Avenue and crossed the street to the Mall, weaving their way through the crowd strolling along its wide green expanse. Laurie was aware of two sources of heat: the bright sunlight on the crown of her head and the sure, possessive hold of Rick's hand on her arm. Between the two, she felt as if she were melting.

Sidestepping lightly, she opened a space between them. Rick's dark glance seemed to measure that distance even as he closed it.

"So, you were telling me about you. How did you go from teaching to a job on the senator's staff?"

With a sigh Laurie abandoned the struggle and matched her step to his. "Well, you could call it Irish nepotism." She smiled. "He and my father are good friends. They were in the Knights of Columbus together long before I was born. And the Royal Order of Hibernians. And St. Patrick's Parish, and—"

"I think I get the picture. A political favor!"

"Actually, more of a medical necessity. Having me under Senator Murphy's wing prevented my father from having a heart attack when I insisted on coming to Washington."

Suddenly Rick stopped in mid-stride and, taking Laurie by both shoulders, turned her to face him. His searching glance swept from her tousled hair over her high, delicate cheekbones, her sweet, expressive mouth, then settled on the deep gray pools of her eyes. His own dark brows drew slowly together.

"Laurie, how old are you?"

Laurie blinked. "Why . . . well, I'm twenty-three. But that's a rather blunt question, don't you think?"

Rick ignored her objection. "That's about what I thought." He frowned. "Are you sure you still want a guardian?"

"It's not just a matter of what I want." Shrugging herself out from between his hands, she arrowed her gaze at his handsome, puzzled face. "I come from a large family, Irish Catholic, full of old spinster aunts and little brothers and sisters. My father always had the last say."

"Always?"

"Yes," she snapped, "under most circumstances. And somehow I was the overprotected daughter. The favorite. The one everyone took care of, cushioned from life's many falls, as if I would break!"

Her voice had risen sharply, and Rick drew close. He fought down a sudden urge to take her in his arms, and settled for a smile. "Hey, it's all right. I can understand someone wanting to take care of you. Loving you that much . . ."

"Oh, Rick, it's more than that." She turned away in frustration. "I'm sorry. There's just too much to explain."

"You want to try me?"

She shook her head, not looking at him.

"Well, what if I promise not to treat you like you're going to break? Will that do? I can't promise not to want to take care of you—"

Her fiery glance made him laugh. He tipped up her chin with one blunt finger. "Whoa, Laurie O'Neill. I'll tell you this: You can take care of *me* any time."

Laurie squeezed her eyes shut and stood absolutely still. The man was impossible! Perhaps all men were, for all she knew, but this one did have a certain dizzying charm!

Lifting one brow, she looked up at his angular features and found her voice. "I think I'm going to spend a little time taking care of myself, thank you very much, Mr. Westin."

"That's all right." He slipped the banjo off his shoulder and laid it gently on the grass. "I can wait; I'm a patient guy. In the meantime, can I make some friendly suggestions?"

"No! Absolutely not!"

"First, you've got to get to know me better. Second"—he held a quieting finger to her lips—"second, go ahead and laugh when you feel like it. Or sing. Or shout. Don't try to hold such a tight rein on your emotions."

"Oh, thank you so much, Dr. Freud!"

"And third"—he ran his hand slowly up her arm—"beneath this damnable uniform of the antilust league, there lies an extremely sensual woman. Why hide her?"

Laurie's mouth flew open as her eyes dropped to the prim navy blue blazer she was wearing. "I . . . wha—what . . . ?"

His laughing dark eyes softened at the startled look on her face. "Ms. O'Neill, we're in the nineteen eighties. They've done away with pantaloons and high button shoes. I can see that Irish beauty of yours lit up like high noon, with a beautiful apple-green silk blouse and a soft skirt that'd swirl about those lovely legs of yours when you walk. And a good hairdresser could do wonders with that shiny coppery hair." His fingers walked seductively up her jacket lapel, brushed lazily against her flushed cheek, and tangled in the uneven strands of her hair.

Laurie stepped back, away from him. "Now . . .

now, stop it, Rick Westin! Since when are . . . are banjo players experts on women's fashion? I have a job, you know, and I don't think they'd like me to come looking like a gypsy or—"

"Or a lovely, ripe woman?" His voice was soft and hushed. "I don't think they'd mind at all, Laurie O'Neill, if you'd slip out of that cocoon you're hiding in."

Her heart was beating wildly against the cage of her ribs, like some panicked bird. This was too much! Too complicated, too unexpected! She didn't know whether what she was feeling was anger or excitement. Didn't know whether to slap his face or melt into his arms. "How dare you?" she managed feebly.

"What?" Confused, Rick narrowed his eyes and stared at her. "How dare I what? Tell you you're lovely? You must know that; plenty of other men must have said it before me."

"No, never!"

"Come on!" he exclaimed disbelievingly. And then he looked at her again and saw her confusion, her vulnerability. Saw in the depths of her gray eyes a new fire that had never been kindled.

"Hey, I didn't mean to upset you," he said softly, hooking his thumbs in the pockets of his jeans. "Listen, sometimes I can be a little brash and presumptuous. But I'm harmless."

Oh, I doubt that, Banjo Man! Laurie retorted silently. But she summoned a smile. "It's okay; it's me. Sometimes I tend to overreact. New situations and things."

"Let me make it up to you," Rick offered quickly. "Tom Preston's going to be in town next week. I'll get tickets and we'll go one night when I'm off."

Laurie lifted her eyebrows. "Who?"

"Preston. The comedian. You know—"

"No, I don't. I don't think I've heard of him."

"Sure you have! Tom Preston . . . the political satirist? The guy Doonesbury envied? He hit every city and campus last year during the election."

"Well, I must have missed him."

"But you couldn't have. *Everyone*, whether you liked him or not, listened to Preston tapes, concerts . . ."

"Everyone but me, I guess," Laurie insisted, sighing with growing frustration.

Rick was looking at her with total amazement. "Come on, darlin', you're puttin' me on!"

Laurie threw her fists against her hips and glared at him. "I am not putting you on! I never heard of Tom Preston, never saw him, never listened to him, and don't care if I do! Now, can we drop this, please?"

Rick's eyes glinted with amused incredulity. "I don't believe it. Where were you, Pittsburgh or Siberia?"

After years on hold, Laurie's Irish temper came to a boil.

Pulling herself up to her full five feet five inches, she threw her shoulders back and faced Rick Westin head on. In a voice that was loud and angry enough to send the pigeons into startled flight, she yelled, "Neither, dammit, Rick Westin! I was in a convent. I was a nun!"

Three

An old man picking up papers with a pointed stick stopped and stared at the irate young woman; a small boy tugged at his mother's hand and pointed her way; three men in business suits halted in mid-conversation to survey the scene.

Rick Westin only stared. His brows moved first, slowly edging up above wide, amazed eyes. Seconds later his voice exploded loud and clear. "You what? Well, I'll be damned!"

"Yes, you may well be!" Laurie retorted quickly, her hands on her hips, her eyes bright with challenge.

"*You* . . . a nun?" He shook his head hard, a nervous half-smile curving his lips. "No . . . no, you can't be a nun. You don't look like a nun. And I held you in my arms and you didn't *feel* like a nun! No, I'd have known—"

"Rick, you're not listening. I *was* a nun. Was. Am not now. Do you understand?"

Scowling, he shook his head again. "Nope. I don't. Why were you a nun? For how long? Why didn't you say anything, instead of letting me make a fool of myself?"

"*Your*self! Of all the insensitive, egotistical things! Here I am, scared half to death, trying to figure out how to talk and act and think like everyone else, like any ordinary person, and you want me to wear a sign saying I used to be a nun, just so you won't be inconvenienced? Well, you can just go . . . Oh, go jump in the Potomac!"

Rick bit back a sudden burst of laughter. "Almost lost your cool, there, woman."

"I am way past losing my cool, *mister!* As if it isn't difficult enough trying to get my life together. You think I wouldn't like to dress more . . . more 'hip'?" she sputtered, yanking angrily at the hem of her neat, tailored blazer. "Well, I would! But the last time I was in a department store, I was buying my high-school graduation dress . . . and I went to an all-girls' Catholic high school!"

"Sh-h-h-h," Rick whispered, slipping an arm around her shoulder and pulling her close. "It's okay, baby, you'll be fine."

"I don't *feel* fine," she snapped, the thread of her argument unraveling within the startling warmth of his arm. "I feel out of time, and out of step."

"Well, I'll tell you, for starters, they don't say 'hip' anymore." His laughter rustled her hair.

"No?" She looked up at him. Her face, clouded with confusion, was suddenly more lovely, more appealing, than any he had ever seen.

Taking hold of her shoulders, he gently turned Laurie to him. His coal-dark eyes held their own confusion as he studied her. "I . . . I don't know how to talk to you now. What to say—what I'm *allowed* to say . . . or do."

Laurie tried to feel the warmth of his hands on her shoulders through the fabric of her clothing. She needed that contact. Needed the warmth of another's touch to give her strength. This was all too difficult. What should she say? What was a woman supposed to say to a man she found irresistibly attractive? She hadn't a clue.

"Rick . . ." She stared up at him, the sunlight revealing golden motes in her wide gray eyes. "Rick, don't ask me."

A muscle jumped in the tense line of his jaw. Dropping his hands to his sides, he whispered harshly, "Of course. I'm sorry. I'm way out of line."

Laurie wanted to cry. This wasn't going well at all! "No!" She groaned, her delicate features crumpling in a frown. "That's not what I meant. I meant 'Don't ask *me*,' not 'Don't *ask* me'! See? Oh, Rick, pretend I've just dropped in from Mars, or the seventeenth century, or something, and I haven't the foggiest notion about . . . about kissing, and all that stuff! But that doesn't mean I wouldn't like to learn. Rick Westin, *you* must know what to do—just go on and do it!"

She stopped to catch her breath, her cheeks flushed, her face tilted up to his in earnest concentration.

Catching her face between his hands, he bent his dark head and kissed her lightly on the lips. His mouth barely grazed hers, so tentative was the touch, but it was filled with a delicious sweetness.

Rick closed his eyes, breathing in the fresh scent of her skin and hair. His fingertips traced the curve of her cheek and ear, so delicate, so perfect.

Laurie stood wide-eyed, rapt beneath his touch. So this was what it felt like! This was a man's kiss, with the musky scent of him filling your head, and the burning heat of him so close. And the promise of life and strength bound within his flesh.

Her breath escaped in a trembling sigh. "Oh . . . my goodness gracious."

"You all right?" he asked softly, his blunt

fingertips stroking her cheeks with incredible tenderness. It was the touch of a man used to loving with his hands.

"I . . . I don't know. I never felt like this before."

Her solemn-eyed candor made him laugh. "Neither have I, darlin'. As the dough told the pastry cook—'I am all you knead!' "

Laurie collapsed against his chest in helpless giggles. "What? Of all the times to be telling a joke—"

"I've been told I'm an unconventional lover." Rick shrugged, the corner of his mouth turning up in a grin.

"Great! What a pair—unconventional and inexperienced!" Laurie laughed. And then she heard what she had said, and the blood rushed to her cheeks. "I mean . . . I *didn't* mean we'd be lovers or . . . oh, heavens! . . . or mean to imply that we . . . we . . ." She struggled to free herself from his embrace, to put some distance between them.

Rick held her tight. "Whoa, darlin'. Don't panic, now. Or faint dead away in the middle of the Mall, or anything. Finding out you were a nun was all the shock my system can take for one day."

He loosened his hold, took a step back, and grabbed his banjo case. "Come on, sweet thing, I'm gonna buy you some lunch. I know a little Chinese place nearby that makes the best steamed dumplings you've ever eaten."

"*Never* eaten," she laughingly corrected him. "We feasted mostly on skinny pork chops and fish in the convent."

"Ah, that again. I think you had better fill me in on the details of your hidden past so I don't make a real fool of myself as we go along."

"Go along where, Westin?" Laurie asked, casting him a quick, nervous glance.

"Down the rocky road of romance, sweet thing. 'Cause that's where we're bound, I can tell."

Stopping in mid-stride, Laurie clasped her hands tightly behind her back and stared at the ground at her feet. "Rick, I . . . I just don't know about any of this. Or even if I want to . . . to get to know anyone just now. My life is in such confusion; maybe it would be easier if we each took our own separate roads for now."

In a hushed, haunting tenor, Rick began to sing:

> *You take the high road,*
> *and I'll take the low road,*
> *and I'll get to Scotland afore ye . . .*
> *but me and my true love will never meet again—*

He stopped, the notes left echoing on the still air, and shook his head, his dark eyes bright with a fierce, restrained emotion.

"Don't you think that would be too sad an ending, darlin'? I've been hurt before, and it may happen again, but I'm sure as hell not going to give up easy."

The passion of the man went through her like an electric shock, shaking her to the bone. There wasn't a thing to say, and no way to resist when he slung his banjo case across his back, took her hand in his, and led her to the restaurant.

Chun Ho's was crowded and noisy, a dim cave of a room with formica tables and wooden chairs, occupied by a surprising assortment of customers: business people with suits and briefcases, diplomats in foreign garb, young mothers with kids in high chairs, a group of punk rockers with dyed hair. A small, round-faced man with spectacles greeted them at the door. "Ah, Mr. Westin. A table for two and banjo?"

He led them to their seats, then winked broadly.

"No playing today, please? I am hoping everyone will eat quickly and leave, so I can fill their places again with other paying customers. I have two sons to put through college, remember?"

"No problem, Ho. I'll keep it in the case." Laughing, Rick explained to a bemused Laurie. "Last time I was in, Ho seated me next to a couple from Tupelo. They had seen the show, and asked for a song. That led to another . . . and three hours later Ho had to throw us all out to get ready for his dinner crowd."

Laurie studied his handsome, expressive face and felt a stirring of surprise . . . and shyness. "I didn't realize I was lunching with a celebrity."

Rick tipped his chair back, his long, jean-clad legs crossed beneath the table, his arms folded over his chest. He gave Laurie a long, calculating look. "You say that as if you didn't like it."

She tossed her coppery hair in denial. "That's not it at all. Everything here's so new to me. I seem to misjudge the importance of things . . . of people. Like a man in the office yesterday afternoon. He came in all grump and growl, and I asked him to kindly sit down and wait quietly until the senator had a free moment. Well, it turned out to be the Secretary of State!"

Rick threw his head back and laughed, the sound so contagious that Laurie found herself laughing along at her own folly. Her cheeks were flushed, her eyes sparkling, and Rick was enjoying the sight and sound of her.

"Well, he probably deserved it!"

"Maybe, but not from me. It's just that I have no feeling yet for all the subtleties, the nuances, of protocol and proper behavior: whom to brush off, whom to favor, whom to—"

"—fawn over? Cater to? Push aside because he's not high up on someone's list? I'd say you're in a state of blessed ignorance, darlin'! You can judge everyone on his own merits—"

"—and lose my job by next Friday!"

"There are other jobs."

"I'm lucky to have this one! There isn't a whole lot of demand in Washington, D.C., for ex-nuns at the moment."

"You'd start a trend!"

Impetuously, Laurie reached across the table and touched Rick's hand. "Are you always so positive about everything?" she asked with a laugh. "So sure and unconquerable?"

He caught her narrow hand with his broad one, weaving his strong, blunt fingers through hers.

"No, but I try like hell. It's the only way I know of to get through this life with grace. But it's not something I thought up on my own."

The stark planes and angles of his face softened with an inward-turning look of memory. "No, Laurie, it's what I've seen. I've ridden my 'cycle out the dusty roads through the hills, and seen old black men sitting on porches, their faces lined with struggle. But they can pick up a banjo, or a mouth harp, and fill the air with the sweet sound of joy. I've seen women in dusty, shapeless clothes, with more babies than they can care for, who can sing a tune that'll make you cry. But they're not cryin'; they're singing about youth and hope and the promise of love, and they make you believe it. I've slept in a shack on a tick mattress stuffed with leaves and feathers and set on a dirt floor, where the table and chairs are finer than store-bought, the wood warm to your touch, rubbed smooth and golden by some man with rough, callused hands. A basket woven so neat you can carry water in it! A song sung so sweet you can think on it and go on for another day."

He swallowed, ran his tongue over dry lips. His

broad chest rose with a sharp, indrawn breath. He let it out with a half-mocking grin. "You've got to watch what you get me started on, sweet thing."

Laurie took a quick gulp of steaming Chinese tea to cover the sudden rush of emotion that shook her. Eyes lowered to the tabletop, she laughed softly. "I'll remember that!"

When she looked up at him from under her gold-tipped lashes, it was with new admiration. "And here I thought you played folk songs in some little café."

"No." Again he flashed that grin that set her heart fluttering. "No, I'm more of a collector. Interpreter. A sort of genuine, single-minded, devil-be-damned roamer of the southern mountains. Just trying to save what I hear, preserve a little of it, so it won't disappear and be lost forever. Some folks do it with paints, with clay or wood; I just do it with songs and stories—a little banjo dancin', a little ridin' to the moon."

"There! You said it again. Tell me, what does that mean?"

Rick leaned forward, elbows on the table, his eyes alive with mischief. "You'll have to come to my show to find out. Will you? Tonight?" Reaching into his shirt pocket, he pulled out a ticket and scrawled his name across the back. "Say you'll come."

"Tonight? Alone? Oh, Rick, I haven't been that adventurous yet. I don't know the city well, and I'm bound to get lost, and I don't know if Ellen's planned dinner. . . ."

"Here." A second ticket materialized. "Bring Ellen. She's seen the show a dozen times, but she won't mind. And if she can't come, well, bring someone else. Female, that is. A girlfriend. I plan to escort you home."

"But I'd have to ride back with whoever brought me; that wouldn't be polite."

"Polite? I'm dyin' here, woman, just trying to figure out how to get you alone for a while, and you're worried about etiquette. You sure know how to make it tough for a guy!"

Honest contrition washed over her face. "But I don't mean to," she answered softly.

Rick felt the breath tighten in his chest. "I was only teasin', Laurie. Just try to come tonight. If you can. Promise?"

Laurie nodded, saved from any further answer by the sudden and welcome appearance of the waiter. In the center of the table he placed a serving platter filled with steaming dumplings. And then, with the care of an artist, he decorated the table with a myriad of tiny bowls, the dipping sauces that transformed the dumplings from sweet to spicy to pungent to piquant.

Wordlessly Rick picked up one set of chopsticks, and deftly demonstrated the proper way to dip and nibble the delicious morsels. A smile of pure ecstasy spread across his face.

Her stomach suddenly rumbling with hunger, Laurie lifted the chopsticks and fished for the first dumpling. It slid halfway across the platter, eluding capture. Frowning, she attacked again, and the dumpling leaped from the table onto her lap.

Rick's rich laughter died beneath Laurie's withering glance. Pulling his upper lip down over his grin, he reached across the table and carefully positioned the chopsticks in her hand, guided her to the platter, tightened the pressure around the tender dumpling, and lifted. The morsel made it halfway to her open mouth before sliding off the end of the chopsticks and across the tabletop.

"Don't laugh," she warned, her gray eyes dancing with silen humor. "I'd like to see what you could do with a string of rosary beads!"

And with that she grabbed a fork and ate her way quickly through a good two-thirds of their lunch.

Rick watched her, his enjoyment of Laurie's nearness almost as sharp a sense as the different tastes on his tongue. When he couldn't resist any longer, he narrowed his dark eyes and broke the easy silence. "Laurie, may I ask you a question?"

Her skin tightened, knowing what was coming, but she nodded, carefully keeping her face empty. "Sure, Rick. What do you want to know?"

"Why did you become a nun?"

She lifted one shoulder, a little-girl gesture that tugged at Rick's heart. "It's not easy to explain now. But then it was so simple. It was expected."

She put down her fork and looked right into his dark, shining eyes, wanting him to understand. "You see, I have three aunts who are in the convent. One, my Aunt Dorothy, is only six years older than I am, and she'd come visit and tell us all— there are five of us kids; I'm the oldest—well, she'd tell us all how wonderful it was, having a life dedicated to God, filled with purpose. She's so good, so . . . so contented, and she'd look at me and say how I reminded her of herself when she was younger, and how she knew I'd love the holy life. . . ." She closed her eyes, silent for a moment, lost in her own thoughts. "My younger sister Katy—well, she was never put in this position; Katy somehow managed to be unmanageable from infancy! And no one ever thought of little Maggie as having a vocation—so that left *me*, Laurie to fulfill those hopes. Anyway, it made my mother and father so happy. So proud. And I thought my own—" The words stopped, trapped behind her white-edged lips.

"Laurie, I'm sorry. If this is too hard, don't—"

"No," she breathed. "It's important that I try to explain. If only to myself." Straightening her shoulders, she continued, "What I started to say was that I thought my own desires and feelings and . . . dreams were wrong and foolish. How could they measure up to this plan everyone seemed to have for me? How dared I say no, when I obviously was being selfish and childish—"

He broke into her words, his voice harsh with anger. "But you *were* only a child! Your dreams should have been nourished, treasured—"

"Rick," she said, brushing away her anger with a smile, "in my big, middle-class, Irish Catholic family, common sense, practicality, tenacity, hard work—those are things to be treasured. Not dreams. But my family meant me no harm."

"Were you harmed?" He asked it softly, his gaze lingering on the faint worry line above her honeyed brows, the solemn set of her delicate jaw, the deep shadows behind her wide gray eyes.

Laurie shook her head earnestly. "No, oh, no. I learned a lot during those years, saw into one part of myself I might never have tried to get to know otherwise. I made many dear friends, rubbed elbows with truly good, fine people. But I could never focus as clearly as I needed to, could never take that leap. I guess it was because"—she hid her smile behind her hand, but not before he had caught a glimpse of it—"I kept dreaming. Even in the convent, when I was trying so hard to adjust, dreams would fill my head at night. And in the daytime, too, when I was walking through the garden on the way to matins, or sitting at a window with the sun spilling through. Or even when I was teaching, when a class went especially well and some eager face would light up with understanding at something I had said. All those times, and so many others, I was filled with the feeling that I had to be part of this life again. Had to leave behind some of those restraints and be free to step back in, open my arms, and take what might come!"

"Whew! You're as bad as I am, darlin'. Ask the right question and we do know how to talk, the two of us."

"You know"—Laurie leaned across the table, grinning, her chin propped on her hand—"I think that was the worst. The single thing that drove me away. The silence. No one to talk to. To hear. To listen. Sometimes I thought I'd explode and go flying into space, whirling in the darkness, searching, searching for someone to understand, to share—"

"Someone to ride to the moon with."

She gulped air in a gasp. "Oh, is that it? Do you feel it too?"

Rick Westin sat quiet for a moment, a hint of surprise and wariness darkening his eyes. Then he smiled and pushed his chair away from the table.

"Come on, I'd better get the check and walk you back. Wouldn't want you to get fired and have to return to your old line of work, now, would we?"

Without thinking, he wrapped an arm cozily around her waist as they started back down the Mall, but then she felt him stiffen and his hand dropped to his side. They walked along for a moment, silent.

Rick ached to touch her, but did he dare?

Laurie craved the warmth and delight of his touch; it was such a newfound pleasure! But now what? Would it all start again, the restraint and isolation, the loneliness? All because she had told him—

Oh, she couldn't stand it! She just couldn't!

Feeling slightly dizzy with desperation, she slipped a hand around his arm, and held on.

Rick grinned, bent his arm to trap her hand

tightly between his forearm and biceps, and strode on with a new jauntiness in his step.

"Slow down!" Laurie laughed, her heart doing happy somersaults.

"Are you kidding? I could leap, dance, kick up my heels, fling up my cap if I had one, Laurie O'Neill! You make me feel good, darlin'."

"I'm feeling none too bad myself, Banjo Man." She giggled, drunk on his excitement. "How do you expect me to work this afternoon?"

"Quickly! And then it'll be evening, and I'll look out into the audience and see your bright, shining face. Promise?"

"I *will* try, Rick. Honest!"

"I'll settle for that. And this." He lowered his face to hers and she felt his breath warm on her lips and then the dizzying pressure of his mouth, sweet and hot and more delicious than anything she had ever known.

And then he flashed that grin. "Ummm, I could get used to this!"

He waved from the corner, a lean, dark-haired man with gypsy eyes and a banjo. Laurie flung her hand up in response, and then fairly danced up the steps of the Rayburn Building.

Four

The Stage Theater always drew a good crowd. But ever since Rick Westin had begun playing there, four years before, there was hardly ever an available seat. Those early audiences had told their friends, and friends had told other friends, and the word had spread. It was a "must" for out-of-town guests. Students from Georgetown caught the metro and rode over just before show time, hoping to take advantage of a last-minute cancellation.

The man had become something of a folk hero.

It was not, Rick privately thought, what you'd expect for a guy who spent half the year riding his 'cycle through the hills and hidden valleys of the Appalachians, wearing worn jeans and work boots, a banjo strapped behind the seat. But what he learned out there, the banjo playing, the ballads, the tall tales and rowdy jokes, the good ghost stories, all were transformed into magic on the stage. The audience loved him. And every night, from November to April, at eight o'clock, things began to sizzle.

At seven fifty-five a cab slid to a stop at the corner of Sixth and Maine.

Laurie was late! She'd die if she had to walk in once the lights were dimmed. Heads would turn. He'd see her!

It was all her own fault! She had spent all evening deciding not to come. Ellen was glued to the phone, hoping for a long-distance call from her boyfriend, Dan. Laurie could think of no one else to ask. Then, at seven, staring at a frozen TV dinner, she had a swift, absolute change of mind. No more hiding, no more saying no to life, no more turning back.

So here she was, in a silk print dress borrowed from Ellen's closet, balancing on a pair of slingback high heels, stuffing a five-dollar bill into the cabbie's hand and not waiting for change.

"Hey, missy, thanks a lot!"

"You're welcome," she called back, and raced to the main entrance.

Handing her ticket to the man at the door, she could feel her heart knocking against her ribs.

He took it, then frowned at her. "I'm sorry, but this isn't for tonight's performance."

Laurie swallowed hard. "What? But . . . but there must be some mistake. Rick . . . I mean, Mr. Westin gave it to me." With an ice-cold hand she reached down and turned the ticket over clumsily. "He signed his name back here, see, and told me—"

"Oh! Sorry, miss. My mistake." He smiled. "Didn't mean to scare you."

"That's okay." She gave a shy little laugh. "I tend to scare easily. And I hated to come in after the curtain was up."

"Curtain? I guess you haven't seen the show before. Go ahead; you're in for a nice surprise."

A young girl with a ponytail met her inside the door and handed her a program. "This way, please." She led Laurie down a narrow hall, down two steps, and into a good-sized, brightly lit room. It was filled with small tables circled by wooden chairs, all occupied by people whose attention was focused on the stage.

On the stage were a single table and chair, and the now-familiar assortment of banjo cases. And Rick.

He was standing stage left, tuning a five-string banjo and talking to a large group seated at a table up front.

The ponytail swung sideways as Laurie's usherette called up to the stage. "Mr. Westin, is this who you were waiting for?"

Laurie froze.

Rick swung their way, grinned, and nodded. "Sure is! Now, folks, we can get started."

There was a hearty round of applause and a few whistles. By then Laurie had melted into her seat, her cheeks aflame, her heart doing cartwheels in her throat.

The lights dimmed and a spotlight caught Rick.

"These first songs are presented exactly as sung by Miss Ada Selves in Hilltop, Kentucky. Miss Ada is ninety-seven, and has a tongue like a whip. She was real particular about my getting the words set down 'jest right,' and believe me, I keep tryin'."

The banjo twanged, and Rick's rich baritone filled the room with "The Wagoner's Lad."

He sang "The Swapping Song" and "The Wayfaring Stranger" and "Cock Robin."

Laurie listened so intently, it was as if she were trying to absorb him through all her senses. Eagerly she took in the husky baritone, the lightning swiftness of his hands on the strings, the lean, dark power of his body as he moved around the stage. The spotlight found sparks in his hair and eyes; his smile beguiled her.

When he stopped playing, she could almost hear the audience's held breath before the applause broke out.

Rick brushed an arm across his brow and grinned. "One summer I was ridin' through Alabama. The bugs were so bad that year, they named the mosquito the state bird." Accepting their laughter with a broad wink, he slung a different banjo over his shoulder and strummed a few chords.

"Now, here's one for that 'fair, pretty lass' who was brave enough to come see me tonight." His dark eyes burned into Laurie's soul. She sat, hypnotized, while all the waves of panic and excitement stilled into a deep, calm pool of happiness.

He sang only to her:

> *Come take my hand,*
> *We'll fly away,*
> *Into the sky, away from here.*
> *On wings of love,*
> *And my sweet tune,*
> *We'll fly to the moon, and linger there.*

Laurie gulped and held her smile steady, but inside she had begun to tremble. Something was stirring, awakening deep within her, unfolding like a bud, a closed hand, a locked heart. It hurt. How much would he ask, this Banjo Man? And how much did she dare?

The rest of the show was a haze through which her turbulent feelings swirled and stormed. Oh, she laughed at the right places, and applauded, and really did hear the sweet, haunting melodies and the rich beauty of his voice. But it was all filtered through her longing and confusion.

She could watch his hands on the strings, and suddenly she'd be seeing them unbuttoning her blouse. She could hear the stamp of his boot heel in time to the music, and suddenly she was imagining the hard shape of his thigh. Just a flash of white teeth behind his grin, and she felt the hot sweetness of his mouth on hers.

She banished the thoughts by picturing the dark notes and scales written on clean white sheets of paper, and was suddenly swept by the thought that she'd want to make love to him in the morning, so that she could see the wonder of him in pale light filtering through the window.

With a groan she sipped her cola, holding the ice in her mouth till her tongue was numb.

Finally the show ended. Amidst a roar of applause, Rick took his bows, his dark, handsome face exultant, his eyes shining. People crowded to the front, asking about songs and places, wanting him to repeat the "jump" line to the ghost stories so they could go home and scare their kids at bedtime the next evening.

And then they left, in groups and couples, all talking and laughing together, like guests invited to a party. The lights began to dim; the ushers straggled in to clean tables and straighten chairs. There was nothing left for Laurie to do but face Rick alone.

He made it easy. Leaping down from the stage, he strode over and caught her in his arms.

"Laurie O'Neill, I am *so* glad you came. Not that I doubted you would." He laughed. "No, not for one second. But boy, was I glad to see you walk through that door! Ummm . . ." He hugged her tight, nuzzling his chin into her neck until she giggled to hide the rush of desire that flooded every part of her. "Oh, you smell so good. Feel so good. And"—he held her away at arm's length while his eyes traveled slowly over her body—"and look so good, all soft and silken."

His words hushed to a whisper against her hair, and for a second Laurie forgot where she was, and felt herself spinning in space.

Then she heard chairs scraping against the floor and the lively chatter of the crew, and she pulled away, laughing. "Hey, you are a crazy man."

"Yup. Crazy. Wild. Wild about you! Can I take you home and nibble on your ear for a while? Just for a day or two?"

"No! Hush!"

"Okay, then how about your nose? Your lips? Your chin?"

Laurie's soft laughter was edged with arousal. "Stop it, Banjo Man! Are you always like this after a show?"

Rick turned to the crew and flung out his arms in mock innocence. "Gang, am I always like this after a show?"

"Yes!" came the chorused reply.

"Don't believe them!" He spun back and caught Laurie around the waist, almost lifting her off her feet. "No, it's you. You have me flyin' high, darlin'! Come on, let's say good night to these traitors and head for my place."

Before she could say a word, Rick had grabbed her hand and led her out of the theater.

The night sky was black and endless, pierced by a million pinpoints of starlight. It hung so close above the quiet city that Laurie was sure she could reach up and touch it. A perfect night.

They walked along in silence for a moment, Laurie's hand curved inside Rick's, enjoying this single point of contact, its innocence and promise.

Rick's voice, husky with desire, broke the stillness. "Will you come home with me?"

Laurie didn't answer.

"We could get a bite to eat. Sit and talk. Whatever you want."

Silence. And the pounding of her heart in her ears.

"Laurie? What do you say, sweet thing?"

"I think I'd better get back to the apartment." Her thin voice sounded strained and sad.

Rick was silent, his brain reeling off arguments, persuasions, often-used lines. He kept them trapped behind his tight, clenched jaw, wanting her, yet knowing how easy it would be to frighten her away.

"Rick, I really do have to go to work tomorrow. And it's late—"

"I know, darlin'. Trouble is, part of me says, 'Go slow, take it easy with her,' and another part of me"—he licked his dry lips—"well, I'm dyin' to take you in my arms and love you!"

The black night air pressed down, heavy and still, upon them. Laurie shivered. She tried to clear the cobwebs from her head, to still the feelings welling up within her.

"Rick, I can't. I'm not ready."

"I know." He drew a deep, harsh breath, filling his head with the cool air, trying to get the earth to steady beneath his feet. "Okay, then, home it is! My Jeep's parked around back. Just ten minutes and you're back safe in your ivory tower."

"Rick!" There was no hiding the hurt in her voice.

"I'm sorry." He squeezed her hand tightly, hating himself. "I am sorry, Laurie. It's late, and I'm beat, and the show gets me wild sometimes."

Leading her to a stripe of moonlight, he stopped, his gaze resting on her face. "Sometimes you have to listen to my words with half an ear, and to my heart for what I'm really saying. 'Always interpret everything in the most favorable sense.' Isn't that a kind of convent maxim, or something?"

"I'm not sure, but I'll take your word for it." She grinned, knowing she was being teased. She cocked her head to one side, meeting his dark glance and feeling the immediate quickening of her pulse. Impulsively she added, "The one thing I do know for sure is that you were great on that stage. I loved the show, Rick; it was wonderful! In fact, *you're* wonderful."

Rick looked down on her face long and hard, his eyes tracing the moonbeams as they played across her smooth cheekbones and danced in the shadows of her hair. The restraint in his voice was tinged with a low and sensual desire. "That is exactly what I intend to prove to you, sweet thing, and not on any stage, either!"

Five

"A guinea pig! A porcupine!" Laurie snapped, glaring at the window in the senator's office.

"What? On Independence Avenue? I don't believe it."

"No, Paula." Laurie groaned, turning around and tugging at her hair with both hands. "No, it's *me*. My hair. I look like a guinea pig that's slept wrong."

Paula yelped with laughter, then settled her face into a more solicitous expression. "Now, dear," she said soothingly, "the color is just gorgeous, but the cut . . . well, it is a bit odd. But then, I don't suppose they have a wide choice of beauticians in a convent."

"Beauticians?" Laurie echoed with a wry grin. "No, this was strictly do-it-yourself haircut time. You'd reach up to feel your hair, and anything long enough to grab, you cut off. At night. In the dark."

"No mirrors?"

"Vanity."

"No long, lazy shampoos and manicures?"

"Sloth."

"Oh, my."

"Oh, my is right! Just look at this mess. I made an appointment for noon at a little beauty parlor near my bus stop, but now I don't think I can even last till lunchtime. It never really bothered me before, but I took a good look at myself over the weekend, and suddenly I can't wait to make some changes." She didn't mention that the self-examination had been prompted by her discussions with Rick.

Paula shook her head, smiling. But she understood the younger woman's sudden self-consciousness. "I know what you mean, dear. First time I found some gray, I rushed out and bought the biggest bottle of hair color I could find."

"Did you feel better . . . prettier?"

"No." Paula grinned. "It turned my hair green. But I do understand. Here"—she reached into a desk drawer and pulled out a small, square kerchief—"if it makes you feel better, you can borrow this until noon. Now, work!"

At five before twelve, Laurie was rushing out the door of the Rayburn Building just as Rick rushed in.

"Oh, excuse me," he apologized automatically, stepping aside to let the strange woman in the babushka go by. Then he did an abrupt double take. "Laurie? What in the world are you doing? I know . . ." He waved her to silence. "It's a costume party, and you're going as a Russian peasant. Lovely! I'll go as Zorba the Greek." He pulled open the front of his shirt, lifted his arms, and did a quick little folk step.

"Funny, Mr. Westin. Very funny," Laurie scolded, narrowing her eyes in mock anger.

"No?" he asked, slipping an arm around her waist.

"No. And you have to let me go. I have an appointment."

"But I want to take you to lunch. There's a new Japanese restaurant just a few blocks away. . . . What appointment?"

"A haircut! I can't stand myself for one minute longer."

"Oh, sweet thing, I could stand you for a moment . . . an hour . . . an eternity."

"Rick!" Laurie blushed furiously, and pressed a finger to his lips.

He kissed her fingertip, smiling gently into her wide gray eyes. Then he lifted both hands and pushed the scarf back off her hair. His thumbs rested on the curves of her cheeks as his fingers wove into the thickness of the burnished strands. "Lovely hair. Lovely woman."

"Not so lovely yet," she whispered, half-mesmerized by the warmth of his touch. "But I'm working on it." Then she shook off his spell and hurried onto the street. "I've got to go! I'm going to be late."

"Where are you going?" he asked, matching her step.

"A little place I found called Carol's Cut 'N' Curl."

"What?" He grabbed her arm, linking his through hers and changing her direction. "You come with me. I'll take you to Larry at Innovations. He does my hair."

Laurie rolled her eyes and grabbed a handful of the dark, wild hair at the back of Rick's neck. "You mean someone *does* this mane? I thought it was untamable."

"I only give that impression," he said, grinning and pulling her close.

*　　*　　*

Innovations was all mirrors and lights, raised plat-forms, and ice-cream colors. The women had billow-ing clouds of hair or short punk cuts, inch-long lacquered nails, and the most beautifully dramatic clothes Laurie had ever seen outside the pages of a magazine. Laurie gulped, smiled shyly, and kept her eyes on Rick's back as he led her through the maze to a raised station set apart at the back of the salon.

He knocked once on the wall. "Larry?"

A handsome man with an enormous moustache poked his head around the corner. "Rick? Hi! What are you doing here?"

Laurie caught a glimpse of a woman's startled face, framed by what seemed like thousands of tiny rollers. She smiled, and the woman smiled back, shrugging lightly.

Rick's next comment caught her full attention. "Larry, this is Laurie O'Neill. A special friend of mine. Think you could fit in a haircut sometime soon?"

"No problem. Mrs. Lehman is almost ready to go under the lights, right, darling? In the meantime Laurie can go change in the dressing room." He pointed imperiously to a small curtained alcove. "Smocks are on the hangers."

They were, and Laurie quickly hung up her skirt, blouse, and blazer and put on a hot-pink, shapeless smock that ended about six inches above her knees. She dashed back across the salon to Larry's station.

At her reappearance, the other woman obedi-ently departed, and Laurie found herself the center of attention.

"Come sit down here." Larry patted the chair, quickly smothered Laurie in a wide plastic cape, and spun her around for a better look. "I say, I think we'll start with a shampoo and some good conditioning, and then we'll see what we've got here. Okay?" he asked, already tipping her toward the sink. "I like to keep my hands on my client's hair from start to finish," he explained. "Lets me get to know the hair intimately, if you know what I mean."

"Yes, of course." Laurie laughed, breathless with a sudden rush of excitement that hit her like a feather pillow right in the stomach. "Yes, whatever you say."

And then there was no way to say anything. There was just the pleasant heat of the water, the cool splash of the shampoo, and the luxurious feel of his strong, practiced hands massaging her scalp. For a second Laurie stiffened, her body reacting with surprised alarm to the almost sensual pleasure. But she couldn't fight it, and the tension that had held her for weeks and months left her, flowing out through the top of her head and away, till she was floating, her eyelids closed, the dark lashes that seemed dipped in gold resting against her pale cheeks.

She was aware of the heat of the water again, and the contrasting chill of the conditioner, but she kept her eyes closed, thinking of nothing. Drifting. The men's voices, Larry's and Rick's, were deep, mellow echoes in the small cubicle, and then Rick began to hum a fragment of a tune, and the sweetness of his voice carried her further away.

It was so peaceful. A peace so simple, so different from the willed, disciplined peace she had spent so long struggling for, in vain.

Her eyes snapped open. "Oh, I almost fell asleep. I'm sorry. . . ."

Larry seemed unaware of her confusion, but Rick smiled, reaching out to tug at the ends of her wet hair. "Hey, just enjoy it. This is going to be fun."

After toweling her hair, Larry stood back, eyeing Laurie with fierce concentration. "Let's see, now," he mused aloud, circling around the chair, studying Laurie from every angle while she frowned and shifted uncomfortably.

"Is it hopeless?" she asked softly, sure that it was.

"Hopeless? Good grief, girl, you sound like you never take a good look in the mirror. *You're* beautiful, but whoever gave you this haircut did the damnedest job I've seen in the ten years I've been cutting hair."

Honesty compelled her to answer. "I . . . I'm afraid I cut it myself, Larry."

"What? Another of those do-it-yourself-ers? The bane of my existence," he growled, his moustache twitching with disapproval.

Laurie met Rick's laughing dark eyes in the mirror. But if he thought she was going to offer any further explanation, he had another think coming! With feigned bravado she tipped up her chin, smiled at her reflection, and tossed back, "That's why I've come to an expert. Do your thing!"

Rick gave her a sexy wink and a silent nod of approval.

Larry picked up his scissors, and Laurie turned her full attention to her own reflection in the glass, curious and excited to see the "new her" emerge.

Larry started in then, snipping and clipping layers of burnished floss, letting the cut hair float to the floor like petals shaken from a flower. A moment's work revealed the shell-like curl of her ear. Another moment and he had bared the pale, vulnerable nape of her neck. Her neck itself seemed longer, a delicate column of translucent skin that begged for a touch, a kiss. His scissors flew, and her high, proud cheekbones were dramatized as surely as if a stroke of color had been applied. He tugged the hair forward over her brow, gave it a swift, shivery cut and let it fall in a bright fringe above her gold-tipped eyelashes.

Laurie felt goose bumps go up her arms. Was this her, this girl being transformed in the mirror? It seemed suddenly impossible. For five long years, there had been no mirror. No girl.

The girl she had been before the convent was a child. A child who spins in a mirror before a school dance, wearing a new dress of pink lace, and thinks she is beautiful. A girl who thinks there will be no end to parties and dances and boys from the prep school across town to pick her up and bring her corsages.

The girl who entered the convent wore a white bride's gown, and then a black habit, and put away mirrors, and memories, and all those foolish feelings. That girl wasn't really a girl anymore; her youth was irrelevant in the timelessness of the convent.

And this girl . . . the one facing her wide-eyed in the mirror now? Could she somehow unlock the child who had been locked away five years ago, find her, free her, and let her grow into a woman? Could this woman be happy? Could she fall in love?

Love. The thought took shape and substance in her mind, and her glance swept immediately to Rick's reflection in the mirror.

"Lookin' good!" he said with a grin.

"Do you really think so?" she asked, her lips parted and her wide eyes shining.

"Oh, yes, darlin', I really do!"

Rick was watching her with a hint of something in his eyes, a touch of awe perhaps. He had thought she was beautiful the first time he saw her, at three A.M. in a dim hallway, so it wasn't just that she was prettier now. No, it was as if he were witnessing some subtle transformation in the mirror. An unfolding of wings. An unfurling of petals. The first bright spark of a fire.

Each clipped, coppery lock that drifted to the floor was a step out into the world. *Into the world . . . and into my heart*, he thought. He felt the swift, sharp stir of arousal that her nearness always awoke in him. Shifting restlessly as he stood, leaning his elbows back against the far edge of the counter, he studied her, thinking, *What power will you have over me when you realize just how much of a woman you are, Ms. Laurie O'Neill?*

As if he had spoken aloud, Laurie blushed. "Stop looking at me like that, Westin. You are making me very nervous!"

"Me too," Larry agreed, brandishing his scissors. "Go away. Go get a soda, or take a walk, or something."

"You two sure know how to hurt a guy," Rick drawled, stretching his lean, hard body. He reached way over his head, hands locked, arching his torso back against the restless tension that tightened his shoulders; the muscles strained visibly against his shirt.

Laurie watched him, feeling the deep, surprising excitement his physical presence caused. Her body responded, and she fidgeted restlessly in her chair.

Rick caught her eye and laughed, a rich, husky sound that mingled with her own silvery laugh. At that moment they were perfectly attuned to each other, like two acrobats hurtling through the air, each one astounded and delighted by the other's perfect timing.

"Am I missing something?" Larry complained, staring at the two of them in amused puzzlement.

"Nothing I could explain." Rick grinned, and Laurie bit at the inside of her cheek, willing back her self-control.

"Good!" was Larry's retort. "Then disappear for about thirty minutes." With a flourish, he resumed his clipping and snipping.

Rick paused on his way out, bent, and picked up one lock of Laurie's shining hair. He tucked it safely in his pocket and left.

In less time than she'd expected, the haircut was complete, and she was spun away from the mirror for a final appraisal.

"Perfect!" Larry confided in a grand stage whisper. "Absolutely perfect." Then, "What do *you* think?" he asked, spinning her back to face her reflection.

Laurie couldn't answer, not only out of modesty, but because her breath was trapped in her throat. The girl . . . the *woman* there in the mirror *was* beautiful. Her hair was a lightly feathered cap of shining copper and gold, thick and rich with highlights, shaped so that it followed the lovely curve of her brow and cheek and neck.

"Well?" Larry prompted, obviously proud of his handiwork.

Laurie nodded her silent agreement. A small smile tipped up the corners of her mouth. "Yes," she said, finding her voice. "It's wonderful. You did a beautiful job! Oh, thank you, Larry." And then, already out of the chair, she added, "I'm going to get dressed before Rick comes back, and surprise him."

"Why don't you go look in our boutique, find something luscious, and *really* surprise him?" Larry suggested, remembering her prim blue blazer.

"Oh, I wish I could, but I don't have time today," she answered wistfully as she picked up her pocketbook and the bill he had written and turned away. But then she hesitated, looking over one shoulder and touching her hand to her hair as if to convince herself that what she saw in the mirror was real. With a shaky laugh, she hurried to the dressing room.

Her clothes were gone. Vanished. And in their place were a soft, silken swirl of a skirt and an apple-green silk blouse.

She dressed in the tiny room, slipped her feet into ivory sling-back sandals that were exactly her size, and turned slowly in front of the mirror. Tears stung her eyes. That man. That crazy, wonderful man. He shouldn't be doing all this; she shouldn't be letting him. But, oh, the sweetness of it! The kindness. The pure dizzying pleasure of being looked at the way he looked at her. How could she resist?

Nothing in her whole life had prepared her for Rick Westin.

And nothing had prepared *him* for the way she looked when she stepped out of the dressing room. Lovely. She glowed with a shy, mysterious awakening that had nothing to do with the haircut or the clothes or anything he had done, and yet he had everything to do with them. Rick felt his heart slam to a stop against his ribs. Something hit him hard behind the knees and smack between the eyes. So this was what had sent the troubadours and minstrels wandering through the countryside with tales of love and maidens fair. This was the secret he had held in his heart as he roamed the Appalachians from spring until fall every year, alone, waiting for someone. Her.

"You look lovely," he said softly.

"Thank you," she said with a shy laugh. Then she shook her head. "I say thank you, and yet I really can't thank you enough. There's no way—"

"There's no need. It's my pleasure. Truly."

He stood looking at her another moment, and she turned slowly before him, suddenly not shy at all. Just happy.

"All right," he said, drawing a deep breath, as though he hadn't breathed for a long time, "all right, let's go get some lunch." He handed her a shopping bag with her old clothes and took her arm, guiding her to the door.

"The bill—" she began.

"I've taken care of everything. And you don't have to thank me. It is my pleasure."

They were halfway down the block when she stopped and turned, pulling him to a halt. "Rick— you make me crazy! I forget who I am, where I am . . . where I'm *supposed* to be! I can't go to lunch now; it's after one. I have to be back at work."

"Okay, then, dinner. I'll pick you up for an early dinner, and then we'll go to the theater, and dancing afterward. Don't say no!" he insisted, waving away her objections. "Listen, the jitterbug is back, and I'm a great jitterbugger. Trust me!"

Six

Didn't that man *ever* sleep? Laurie yawned languidly, rubbing the heels of her palms against her eyes.

She pulled her chair over to the window and leaned across the sill. The white light of early morning washed across her arms, but there was no warmth to it yet, just a teasing promise. Since last night, all of life seemed a teasing promise: a golden ring on the merry-go-round, a surprise at the bottom of the Cracker Jacks box.

She hadn't slept a wink and was sorry now, at just past seven A.M., with the whole day stretching ahead. Her eyelids drooped over sleepy gray eyes; the small of her back ached; her heart thumped and bumped unevenly in her chest, a tom-tom beating out a disquieting message.

Rick Westin! There was the heart of the problem.

The thought of him pulled at her soul like the tide, constant and irresistible. When she closed her eyes, his face was imprinted on her lids; when she drifted into a moment's sleep, he moved through her dreams.

They had shared an exquisite Japanese dinner, seated on woven cushions behind a paper screen, drinking warm sake that made her head spin. Or was it the look in his dark eyes that made her dizzy? Then they'd made a mad dash to the theater, where she had sat at what was now *her* table, stage front, to be thrilled again by the sound of his voice and the wild, dark excitement of him on stage. And as if that weren't enough, later they had gone dancing at some little club where the band members all knew Rick and the music tugged at their feet . . . and she wished he would hold her in his arms forever.

And then she had sat awake in the stiff kitchen chair for most of the night, trying to talk some sense to herself.

The trouble was, she wasn't listening.

She was, quite honestly, crazy about the man. She wanted to quit her job, abandon her bed on the couch, snatch up her hairbrush and toothbrush, and go pound down his door. She could see the headlines now:

EX-NUN ARRESTED FOR BREAKING AND
ENTERING LOVER'S APARTMENT!

Hugging her knees, she pressed her fevered forehead against the windowpane. She couldn't believe herself, talking about a lover! A month ago she would have been just leaving the chapel after matins, her veil in place, her dark skirt brushing the floor. Too much was happening. Too much, too fast. It was wonderful—but so very confusing.

Again she closed her eyes and saw his dark, angular face, the curve of his jaw, the shape of his mouth. She pictured his wild, dark hair and gypsy eyes, the sexy grin that flickered across that perfect face.

Oh . . . was this love? Could it be? She had so little knowledge, and no practice at all. How was she supposed to be sure? Whom could she ask?

"Good grief, what are you doing up already?" Ellen stormed in through the front door, her eyes taking in everything at once, as always. "Honestly, a person who doesn't have to be at work until nine should sleep till at least eight forty-five! Coffee on?" she asked without pausing for breath.

"Gee, I forgot. I'm sorry."

"No problem. I'll have it perking in a sec. Should I put a muffin on for you?"

"No, thanks, I—"

"Hey, are you all right, kiddo? These last few days you've had the appetite of a sparrow! And you know, you're looking very pale . . . kind of translucent, you know what I mean? Like a candle burning at both ends. Have you got a fever?"

Before Laurie could protest, Ellen was perched on the windowsill, one palm resting flat against Laurie's forehead, the other hand circling her wrist. "Uh-oh, just as I expected. Temperature elevated, pulse erratic; I bet your blood pressure's sky-high. Did you have a good time last night?"

Laurie had to laugh at the obvious non sequitur. "Thank you, Nurse Farrell. It's nice to know you make house calls."

"Anything for a friend. So tell me, how's Rick Westin?"

"He's fine," Laurie said, taking a sudden interest in the sunrise.

"Aha!" Ellen chortled with delight. "Pulse racing! Pressure mounting—"

"Ellen, stop it." Laurie laughed, jumping off the chair and out of reach. "You're supposed to be on *my* side."

"But I am! I'm hoping you fall madly in love with the fellow, because he's the nicest man I've ever met. And you're my best friend. The two of you deserve each other. Besides"—her hearty laugh bounced off the walls—"it'll be a wild and crazy love affair, that's for sure! I could write it up for *Woman's Day* and make a fortune."

"Ellen!"

"No, I'd never do that. I promise." She held up three fingers in the Girl Scout oath, and then added with a wink, "But I am anxiously awaiting confirmation of my diagnosis."

Laurie avoided her friend's eyes, turning away with her hands clasped behind her back. "The patient isn't sure herself yet."

"Ah, understandable, considering the patient's recent case history."

Laurie licked her suddenly dry lips. "Is it your considered opinion that the patient could survive exposure to such a disease?"

"Oh, sweetie"—Ellen stepped closer—"it's life that's the disease. Love is the cure."

Later, standing beneath the hot spray of the shower, Laurie tipped back her head and let the water wash over her upturned face. But instead of soothing her, the water's rush added to her restlessness. She felt fidgety, itchy, all in a dither! Out of nowhere a scene from an old western movie popped into her head: a captive tied up on top of a red-ant hill. That was just how she felt! It was as if her skin were alive, every nerve ending aflame, every synapse relaying a single message over and over again: *desire.*

His kiss. His touch. The heat of his body.

She wanted Rick Westin.

But if she got him, what in the world would she do with him?

Laurie dissolved into heated laughter, and turned the cold water on full force. There had to be some calm, logical, mature way to deal with this entire situation. Trouble was, she couldn't think of a thing.

She turned off the water, stepped from the shower, and covered herself with a fluffy terry towel. Rubbing herself dry, she was suddenly and totally aware of her body and its own secret, teasing promise.

What would it be like to make love with a man? What would he think of her body, these narrow shoulders and small, pink-tipped breasts, these hips? Were her hips too bony to be provocative? Were her buttocks too flat? Did men like that, or did they want full, curving bottoms to cup in their hands? And her knees . . . and her feet . . . and the parts of her body she was carefully not naming, not even to herself! Could she ever let a man look at her naked?

The thought sent horrified shivers racing down her spine from her reeling brain.

But her traitorous body was busy with its own fantasy. Her heart was turning somersaults in her throat, her stomach was tied in a knot, and her skin was covered with a light sheen of sweat. *Naked.* What would it be like to stand in front of a man naked? Or in front of a naked man?

No sooner thought than imagined! With her mind's eye she saw Rick Westin, with his dark, flashing eyes and the now-familiar smile tugging at his lips. And what else? Well, he had broad shoulders, and dark hair on his chest. But was there a lot? Just a little? She had been too scared to notice. Which would she like better? And his chest was tanned and solid, the muscles as well defined and beautiful as those on some Greek statue. And all that muscle tapered down to those slim hips that she had to keep her eyes off when he wore his tight, faded jeans. She had seen no more than that, but she was sure he'd have rock-hard calves, and strong, solid thighs and . . . oh!

She let her forehead rest against the steamed glass of the mirror and squeezed her eyes shut tight. Heavens! Another complication. If she couldn't think sexy, she sure couldn't *do* sexy. But she wanted to.

Yes! If the truth be told, which it might as well be, she, Laurie Bridget Margaret O'Neill, wanted to think and do and be sexy! And whether it made any sense or not, she wanted to think and do and be it with that wild, wonderful banjo man.

And with a toss of her head and just one skeptical glance back into the mirror, she dressed for work and rejoined Ellen in the kitchen.

"Finally! I was beginning to wonder if I was ever going to get my bathroom back. And after downing three cups of coffee all by my lonesome, I need it!"

Laurie was instantly repentant. "Ellen, I'm sorry—"

"Laurie! I'm just joking. Don't apologize!"

"Sorry—"

"Yikes! There you go again." Rolling her eyes heavenward, Ellen sighed. "Laurie, stop it. Do not apologize for every breath you take. Laugh a little at life. You need to step away from being Sister Loretta Ann; let Laurie live her own life."

Dark color mottled Laurie's cheeks. "Yes, I'm not a Sister. I don't feel like a Sister. And—"

"And you don't look like a Sister! That's some gorgeous outfit you left draped across the dining-room chair. Not what you went out in yesterday morning, is it?" she asked with more than a hint of a grin.

"No, I . . . or rather Rick bought it for me in a boutique yesterday while I was having my hair cut."

"Which *also* looks very unnunlike, Sister Loretta Ann."

"Oh, don't *do that*, please, Ellen."

"Uh-oh . . . I can tell from the way you wrinkle your nose, I'm in trouble. You know, you used to do that all the time when we were kids; that was how I could tell you were really mad at me when I broke your doll carriage or knocked your goldfish bowl off the desk."

An affectionate smile crinkled the corners of Laurie's eyes. "I really was quite fond of Rhett and Scarlett, and it was terrible to see them flopping around on Mama's rug. But I forgave you!"

"Good. Then you'll forgive me for whatever goof I just made."

"Of course, silly. It's just that it makes me very uncomfortable to hear you make fun of the convent. There were some good things about those years."

"I wouldn't know. But," Ellen added quickly, "we did have a different way of looking at things, even then. So it's my turn to apologize. Now, can we get on to breakfast? If the flame's gonna burn, we'd better feed it some fuel."

Lazily, she strolled to the toaster and popped in an English muffin.

From her chair at the kitchen table, Laurie asked softly, "Ellen, if I did happen to care about Rick—I'm not saying I do, just 'if'—what should I do?"

"Honey, I'm the last one in the world to tell you that." She turned with a shrug, wiping her hands on a dish towel. "I was crazy about him when I first met him. I hoped something might come of it—and don't you start apologizing again, because now I've got Dan—but it didn't. I'm not what Rick Westin was dreaming of on those long rides through the hills. But if *you* are, then it's because there's something special inside you. All you'll have to do is let it out, let it shine. He'll show you how. That man is something else."

"That's what frightens me."

Ellen fixed her with an impatient look. "Well, you can run away and hide, or you can open your arms to one of life's rare blessings. It's up to you." Turning her back, she speared the muffin on the prongs of a fork. "Here."

"Thank you. Ellen . . . have I done something to make you angry?"

"Nothing. Listen, I'm just a grump. It's been a tough couple of nights in the E.R."

"Nothing else?"

"Oh, some problems with Dan; no phone call, and small things like that." She shrugged dispiritedly. "But that's another story, and you're going to be late if you don't get moving. I'll see you tonight." And without another word of explanation she disappeared into the bedroom.

Laurie felt as if she were carrying the weight of the world on her shoulders as she walked down the halls of the Rayburn Building. Emotion. Contact. Involvement. That was what she had fled the convent to find. But how in the world was she ever going to handle it all?

It was a relief to push open the door to the senator's office, find her own neat, orderly desk, and get to work. For the past three days she had been researching a piece of legislation concerning student loans, going back over case histories through the years, writing summaries from which the senator could draw his own conclusions. It was work that demanded total concentration, a blessed escape from the turmoil of her own thoughts.

The hours droned by, and when Paula poked her head in the door mid-afternoon to offer an invitation for lunch, Laurie waved her on.

"Thanks, but I'm going to pass today. I've almost got this finished. And—"

"Oh, come on, Laurie. We've both worked straight through for hours, and the good senator does not pay overtime. Besides, I'd enjoy some company."

"No, not this time," Laurie demurred. And then, afraid she'd hurt Paula's feelings, she admitted, "I'm doing my ostrich routine: keeping my head buried in the books so I don't have to think! Paula, sometimes I wonder if I have enough grit, or stamina, or something, for life."

"Age, that's all it is, Laurie. You're young and, well, particularly sensitive. You're a caring, honest young woman, and that's good, but painful at times; it makes you vulnerable. The years will give you a harder shell, whether you like it or not."

"Happen to know any place to order temporary shells, quick?" Laurie begged wide-eyed.

"I'm afraid not, dear." Paula smiled. "Except for a sense of humor. Sometimes you've got to look life in the eye and laugh." With a twinkle in *her* eye she sauntered over and perched on the corner of Laurie's desk. "Have you heard the one about the traveling salesman?"

"*I* haven't," a husky baritone interrupted from the doorway. "But I'm ready!"

Rick stepped into the room, bringing an invisible electricity with him. The whole room seemed to hum.

"Glad to see me?"

Laurie wiped the palm of one hand across her

brow, hoping to hide the excitement that surged through her at the sight of him.

In that second of silence, Rick cocked his hands against his lean hips and lifted one dark brow. "That question is not supposed to take any thought, Laurie O'Neill. The answer is 'Of course, Rick! When we're not together, the hours seem like days, the days weeks!' "

"Rick!" She shot a nervous glance at Paula, hushing him.

"Sorry, but Paula can tell I'm hopeless."

"A hopeless romantic," the older woman chided with obvious fondness for the rash young banjo player. Apparently they had become firm friends during their conversation the week before. "Laurie, answer the man's question."

"Oh, you two! What is this, a conspiracy?"

"Yup."

Deciding to join the game, Laurie pursed her lips and looked up at Rick from under her lashes. "Now, what was the question?"

In one swift movement he was behind her chair, his cheek close to hers, his breath a whisper in her ear. "I am crazy about you, sweet thing."

Goose bumps traveled across her flesh. "You are crazy. Period."

"Crazed with desire. Twanging like a banjo string that's strung too tight. Pushed to the brink. Dangerous . . ."

"Well, folks, time for me to call it a day," Paula quipped, turning on her heel and heading for the door. "I'll see you Monday, Laurie. Have fun. And laugh—"

"Paula! Oh, Rick, look what you've done. She and I were just about to go out for a late lunch, and . . . well, that is, we were considering a late lunch, and—"

"It's all right, Laurie," he said softly, brushing

the backs of his fingers slowly down her cheek, "we'll take her to lunch another day. Promise. But today we wouldn't have time."

"Why not? What are we doing?" She could barely hear her own voice above the pounding of her heart.

Carefully keeping his fingers in contact with her skin, he swung around in front of her, his lean, hard body filling the narrow space between her knees and her desk. His face was inches from hers, his dark eyes shining. "We're going to Philadelphia for the weekend. You know, home of the Liberty Bell. I'm doing a fund-raising concert for the University of Pennsylvania tomorrow afternoon."

"Have a nice trip, Mr. Westin," she croaked.

"Uh-uh. *We're* going to have a nice trip."

"Oh, no, we're not! I could never do that; I mean, what would I tell Ellen? And where would I stay?"

"With me."

"You are crazy! I couldn't do that. I . . . I'm—"

"—a beautiful woman. That's what I see when I look at you, Laurie O'Neill. I see the fire in these wide eyes, the stubborn tilt of this chin, the fine strength of the delicate bones beneath your silken skin. Don't blush, it's the truth. It's that gentle courage that's got me falling in love with you."

"Courage! I'm the world's biggest chicken," she insisted, doing a terrible imitation of a cackle and flapping her elbows.

A sure smile leaped from his lips to his dark, blazing eyes. "You're wasting your time, woman. Come on; we've got to get going."

His hand circled her back, its warm, firm pressure lifting her from her seat.

Laurie let herself be led almost to the door, then stopped short, her heels digging into the carpet. "Whoa . . . wait a minute! What . . . what did you say about falling in love?"

His rich laughter curled around her heart. "You heard me. I am falling in love with you, Laurie O'Neill. And much to my surprise, I like it. I may even write a song about you."

"Oh, no!" She groaned, leaning back against the circle of his arm. "That's my reward for getting mixed up with a banjo man! Rick Westin, promise me you won't sing any song about me in front of other people."

"Sing it?" he repeated, his voice soft and full of tenderness. "I'd shout it from the highest hill, send it echoing to the stars."

He lowered his face to hers and kissed her with a fierce and yearning desire. His mouth moved across hers with bruising force, hot and sweet. And she answered, tentatively at first, and then with eager and unabashed response. She had never felt anything like this before, as if her lips were ablaze, all her swirling emotions centered there beneath the heat of his kiss. His mouth pressed hard against hers, lifted, and then pressed down again. He was tasting her, savoring the satin smoothness of her lips.

"Rick. Oh, Rick." She was melting in his arms. When her knees gave way, she let her weight fall forward against him, her reed-slim body cradled within the hard bow of his hips. His body drew her like gravity, and she clung to him, wrapping her arms around his neck, stroking the dark mane of his hair.

His tongue slipped between her parted lips, seeking the sweet moisture of her mouth. And she felt something stir deep within her, an unknown emotion that rose in an aching curve like some primeval tide. A wave of passion swept through her, shattering the boundaries of all she had known and accepted. And her body awoke from its long sleep.

Seven

"Sleep! That's what I'm talking about, Mr. Westin! Where am I going to *sleep*?"

"Why don't we wait until we check in? We can go up and see the room. I asked for two queen-sized beds, so you'll be farther away from me there than we've been in the Jeep for the past four hours! Hey, we'll practically need a phone to talk to each other—"

"No, Rick! I mean it. No!" Her voice dropped as several hotel guests glanced up from behind their newspapers to stare at the blushing young woman standing in the middle of the lobby. "Rick, my head's spinning. I mean, look at me—I don't know how we even got to Philadelphia! The last thing I remember is being bundled into a Jeep and whisked away without so much as an overnight case! I think you slipped me something in that kiss!"

"Damn right I did! Want to see it again?" He wrapped his arms around her and bent his dark head toward hers.

Laurie buried her face against his shoulder and laughed. "Not here—and not now! I want you to please step up to that desk clerk and get me a room. A single room with a single bed. Rick . . . I . . . I just couldn't consider any other arrangement. Good grief, I don't even have pajamas."

Her wide gray eyes were filled with a silent plea for understanding; confusion and pain swam in their lambent depths, and Rick felt his heart hammer against the wall of his chest. He could never hurt her.

"Okay, sweet thing. Let me see what I can do."

With his arm around her shoulder, they approached the reservations clerk. "Hi, I'm Rick Westin. I have a room held for tonight."

"Yes, Mr. Westin," the girl answered, checking the information on her computer terminal. "That's room 721. The bellboy will take your luggage up."

"One problem. I need a second room, please. Nearby if possible."

The girl swung her gaze from his appealing face to Laurie's and back again. "I'm sorry, sir, but there isn't a room left in the hotel. Not one for miles; the town is filled with conventions and music-loving alumni over at the university—which is partially your fault!"

"Thanks." He flashed a rueful grin. "Right now I could use one less fan!"

"I'm sorry." She handed him a key, then frowned back at the screen. "Oh, no, I have to apologize again. There wasn't a room left with two beds, but this does have a couch. I mean, if that helps . . ." Lifting her brows, she looked hopefully at Laurie.

Laurie swallowed around the growing lump in her throat. "That will be fine. We'll manage, thank you."

Pocketing the key, Rick followed the bellboy's retreating back toward the elevator.

Laurie trailed behind, her thoughts racing. What was she going to do? Alone in that hotel room with Rick, they'd end up in bed. In bed. In each other's arms. Making love.

And she couldn't. She just couldn't. Not that she didn't want to! Oh, that fierce ache was back, curling in her loins, riveting her thoughts to her desires, so that her whole body curved toward his like some trembling green leaf curving toward the sun. Oh, she wanted him. Wanted him to love her. Wanted their loving to make them one.

But she mustn't, mustn't give in!

For her, it was too soon. They hadn't talked about any kind of a commitment, about a long-term relationship. That, above all, was the problem; Laurie O'Neill did not want to fall headlong into another commitment right now. She couldn't, not until she had sorted out her feelings and gotten her new life in order.

The elevator door slid open. Rick turned with restrained eagerness and held out his hand.

With a silent prayer, Laurie slipped her ice-cold hand into his. For someone who had spent five long years striving for self-discipline, she was a dismal failure. Alone in that room she would yield.

The room itself conspired against her. Decorated in soft pastels, it boasted a broad, king-sized bed and an impossibly tiny "couch" that didn't even deserve to be called a love seat.

When Laurie groaned, Rick playfully ruffled her hair. "Take it easy, sweet thing, I'm not going to attack you if you don't want me to. I'll just sit here and gnaw the legs off the furniture."

Wrapping her arms around his back, Laurie hugged him close. "Oh, Rick, how do you put up with me?"

"I don't know!" he teased, burying his face in the shining floss of her hair. "Ummmm . . . you smell like flowers in early spring, lilacs and honey-suckle." His eyes closed and he rested his chin on the top of her head, breathing deeply. "Laurie, I don't understand all this any more than you do. I've had plenty of sex, but sex isn't love. And that I *haven't* had. We're starting even, you and I. And yet I know, as sure as I'm breathing, as sure as that sun's gonna set and the moon's gonna rise, I know you are the one I've been waiting for. Don't ask me how. But it's as if, when I look in your eyes, I see my own soul."

Laurie edged away, pushing her hands flat against his chest to get some space between them, some air back into her lungs. Suddenly she couldn't breathe. "Rick," she said, gasping, "what if this isn't love? What if it's a mistake? I've made them before!"

Rick threw back his head and laughed, knowing how impossible that was. "Here," he said, taking hold of the thin, cold hand that fluttered against his chest and pressing it to his cheek. "See this face? That's no mistake. And here." He held her hand hard against his chest. "Feel this heart? That's no mistake! And here." He slid her hand down until it was pressed against the flat muscle of his belly. "This body is no mistake, with all its needs and desires. This is real. This is life, and love."

"But maybe it's lust!"

"Oh, Lord, you are wonderful!" His laughter rumbled into a growl in his throat. "*This* is lust."

He lifted her in his arms, turned, and tossed her onto the bed. In the same swift movement he was on top of her, straddling her body, his knees planted on either side of her thighs, his lips nibbling at the hollow of her throat. He kissed her neck and face and ears, quickly, playfully, his teasing mouth and words coaxing giggles from her even as she wiggled away.

"That, Laurie O'Neill, is lust," he said, rocking back on his heels at the foot of the bed.

She clutched a pillow to her chest and grinned at him, poised for flight, her lower lip caught between her teeth.

He grinned back, the sweat standing on his brow and at the open collar of his shirt. His voice was a soft, throaty whisper. "But, darlin', what happens later—when you're ready—that's love."

Sudden tears stung Laurie's eyes, and she nodded without answering.

Rick sat for a moment, letting the heaving of his chest subside, and then he stood. "I'm going to take a shower, Laurie. There's a short rehearsal at eight, and then we can grab some dinner. Okay?"

"Sounds fine," she whispered, weak with desire.

"Okay!" With a wink he disappeared into the bathroom.

Laurie sat at the head of the bed, leaning against the wall, as limp as a rag doll. Fainting seemed like a nice option. Why couldn't she just swoon away, wake up tomorrow, and never know what had happened?

Instead her thoughts bounced back and forth like Ping-Pong balls. Stay. Go. Make love. Run away. Stay. Hide. What should she do? If only there were someone to tell her, but who? Who could tell her what to do?

Only your own conscience, came the reply.

Like an obedient child she pulled open the night table drawer, took out the phone book, and leafed through it. She'd do what she should have done in the very beginning. The call took only a moment, and she marked the address neatly on the little bedside note pad provided by the management.

When Rick stepped out of the bathroom, a towel

wrapped around his hips, his chest and legs bronzed and gleaming, the dark hair curling damply against his skin, she was standing near the door, her pocketbook over her shoulder.

His smile vanished, one dark brow swooping low over a narrowed eye. "What's up?" he asked. "Where are you going?"

Feeling her heart twist, she answered lightly, "You're not going to believe it. I had a friend in the convent who left and moved to Philadelphia. I took a chance and gave her a call. And she was home." Forcing a bright smile, she weathered his dark silence and went on lightly. "Well, she's just dying to see me."

"I bet she is."

"She is," Laurie insisted, smiling even more brightly. "And since you had a rehearsal, I thought I'd catch a cab and go on over. I'll see you later."

"For dinner?"

"I'll try. But if I'm late, just have something without me."

A flicker of pain shadowed his eyes. "I'll wait."

"No! Oh, all right," she stuttered, shifting the strap on her shoulder. "I'll see you later."

"Do you want to wait a few minutes, so we could at least ride together as far as the campus?" He searched her face and then licked his dry lips. "No, huh?"

"We'll be going in opposite directions, I think," she said, her eyes on the floor.

"I guess so," he answered. Then he looked at her for a long, silent moment.

Fidgeting under his stare, she raised her eyes and saw the way his dark, wet hair clung to his head and curled just slightly against the back of his neck. Rivulets of water traced paths across the tensed, straining muscles in his shoulders and chest. His skin was all golden and gleaming, so foreign and yet already so familiar and beloved.

Tears brimming in her eyes, she met his gaze, then quickly looked away. " 'Bye," she said, and closed the door behind her.

The drive to the YWCA took thirty minutes, and she sobbed noisily in the back of the cab during the entire trip.

"Lady, are you okay?" the cabbie asked as he pulled to a stop in front of the old brick building.

"Yes, of course," she answered, sniffing loudly.

"You sure?" came the gruff response.

"Yes, I said. I just saw a terribly sad movie—"

"In the *hotel?*"

"Yes! It was a made-for-TV movie, okay?"

"No skin off my nose, dearie. You just look like hell."

"Well, thank you, sir," Laurie snapped, her temper saving her from despair. "Now, if you'll just tell me how much I owe you—"

"Fifteen dollars even. And here's some free advice: if you decide to go back to the hotel to, uh, see the end of that movie, call a cab from inside. You wouldn't want to be standing out on the street by yourself at night."

"I have no intention of going anywhere."

"Good. But if you should change your mind, call 555–6000 and let them radio me; name's Frank."

Inside, the dour old woman behind the desk gave Laurie a key, and instructed her not to leave her floor to fraternize with men.

Slowly Laurie climbed the two dim, echoing stairways to room number 303. Inside was a narrow bed, an old chipped dresser, and a dingy window. It was silent and empty and painfully lonely. She went to turn the lock on the door and it slipped between her fingers, broken.

Laurie sat on the edge of the bed and stared at

the peeling walls while a television movie droned on.

She was miserable.

Noises in the hallway were tinny and unfriendly: doors slamming, strangers shuffling past in the hall. Briskly rubbing her arms, she tried to banish the tiny shivers of fear and loneliness that plagued her.

What was she doing here? Why was she here? Whom was she punishing?

Carefully, painfully, she went over every moment of the day from Rick's appearance in the doorway at the senator's office. Their kiss. The long Jeep ride. The hotel room. What was so terrible about it all? What had frightened her so that she had fled here, back to a tiny room and a narrow bed and loneliness?

Was she afraid of happiness?

Thinking back, she realized this had been the happiest, most carefree, most loving day of her life. Now the day felt hollow, broken. Before, with Rick, it had been full, but now it was empty. Empty room. Empty heart. Empty hands folded in her lap.

And yet her hands remembered the feel of his hair. Her arms remembered the shape and heat of his body. Her senses remembered the feel and taste and smell of him. She wanted that. She did!

Then why run away?

Because in life there was only going forward or going back.

Back was safe and known . . . and lonely.

But forward was a mystery that had her running and hiding. She didn't know anything about sex, about sensuality! How did you touch someone else? How did you let someone touch you without bursting into flame? All day she had burned with new feelings that frightened her. She felt like a butterfly just out of the cocoon, a baby bird pushed from the nest.

"Cut the poetry, O'Neill, and figure out what you're doing before it's too late!" She groaned aloud, and then gulped in surprise.

How many nights had she stood in her convent room, thinking aloud, just like this? Thinking, and praying, and wishing for happiness.

And here it was!

So what if she hadn't known happiness would be wearing faded jeans and playing the banjo. Call it beginner's luck!

Several minutes later Laurie hurried back down the stairs, her heels clattering on the linoleum, and came to a sharp stop in front of the desk.

"Excuse me? Ma'am? I'm checking out."

"You just checked in."

"I know," Laurie replied sheepishly, "but I've had a change of heart."

"There are no refunds."

"That's okay. I didn't expect my money back. I just wanted you to know the room was empty."

The woman looked at her, pressing stray wisps of hair back into her bun with a dry, thin hand. "Fine."

Laurie was about to smile, then decided to save it for someone else. "Can you tell me where there's a pay phone?"

"In the corner."

Laurie dropped in her coins and punched the numbers. "Hi. Could you please send Frank to pick up a fare at the 'Y'? He's expecting the call. Thanks."

When they pulled up in front of Rick's hotel, Laurie gave Frank the smile she had been saving and a five-dollar tip.

He shook his head. "You know, with what you spent on cab fare tonight, you and your fella could've stayed at the Hyatt!"

"That's all right." She laughed. "This is where I want to be. And Frank . . . thanks for everything."

Laurie slammed the taxi door, waved, and hurried into the hotel hobby, her skirt twirling about her knees.

The elevator was stopped at the sixth floor and the call button was already lit, but she pushed it anyway, willing it to hurry.

After ten heartbeats she couldn't stand it any longer and pushed the button again, trembling with impatience.

What if he wasn't there? What if he was sick to death of her uncertainty, her naivete? What if he had taken her advice and gone out somewhere for dinner . . . or met someone? He must know dozens of people in this town, and at least half would be women, all sexier and more sophisticated than she. And each and every one would probably have been glad to take Rick Westin out to dinner—or home!

She was so nervous she couldn't stand still. Her eyes clung to the lights above the door, counting the numbers down to "lobby." When the door slid open she jumped inside, hit "7," and stood with her toes at the door as the elevator rose, her arms folded tight across her chest, as if to keep her heart from leaping clear out of her body.

She raced down the hall to 721 and tried the knob, then knocked loudly.

"Rick—Rick, it's me . . . Laurie!"

The door was yanked open from inside, and he was there. He took one eager step toward her, then held himself back, his dark eyes studying her face. "Hi, darlin'," he said softly, his hand resting, white-knuckled, on the doorknob.

For a second Laurie couldn't say anything. Her head was suddenly empty of words, filled instead with the sight of him in fawn-colored slacks and a pale blue knit shirt, his face and body so beautiful, so beloved. Then she lifted both shoulders in a half-embarrassed shrug and smiled at him. "I'm back."

"I'm glad," he answered, and caught her in his arms.

His kiss was hot and passionate, and said all he didn't say in words. How much he wanted her. How much he needed her. How much the evening had cost him. Her lips snagged like silk against the rough hunger of his mouth.

"I thought I'd lost you," he said, then groaned when he finally regained a semblance of control. Pushing his fingers through the soft spill of her hair, he tipped her head back so he could look into her eyes. "Where did you go?"

"You mean you didn't buy my convent story?" she whispered, tracing the outline of his lips slowly with her fingertips.

"Not for a moment," he answered, nipping gently at her fingers. "You're a terrible liar; those eyes give you away."

"Then why didn't you stop me?"

"Could I have?" he asked, his hand shaping itself to the curve of her cheek.

"No, I was too scared."

"Of what, darlin'? Not me!"

"Yes, you! You don't know what you do to me! Now, stop it! Don't you dare laugh—no, not even grin!—and *certainly* don't look at me with that wild glint in your eye." She smoothed the rough, dark hair back from his brow. "Oh, Banjo Man, you're changing my whole life: how I think, how I feel . . . it's scary. All of a sudden I felt as if you were some incredibly powerful magnet, and I was nothing but tiny bits of steel, jumping, wiggling, in your direction, and I was totally out of control. My body just took over with all these strange feelings, and . . . and—"

"It's all right, sweet thing. I was feeling the same way. But I knew you didn't know that yet."

He laughed softly into her hair, filling his head with the sweet scent of her. "Laurie, I can tell by the way you look at me, you think I've got the secret; you think I've got it all wrapped up and tucked in my pocket. But I don't. Not with you. You've got me turned inside out."

She moaned softly. "Then what are we going to do, Rick?"

"We're going to let it happen, Laurie. I'm already in love with you . . . and you, you're falling in love with me. I'm willing to stake my life on it. I know it scares you; it has to!"

"But I don't know *how*. I don't know if I can handle anything more right now than untangling my own life. I don't know anything!"

"Oh, yes, you do! You know how to be gentle and loving and caring. You know how to be open and honest. You listen to me and it's like you're hearing the thoughts in my head, the things I can't always say. And you look at me with those incredible eyes and it's like you're seeing the man I really am, the man I can't always show the world. You know all that—I'll teach you the rest."

Standing on tiptoe, she kissed him lightly on the mouth. "Well, I'll try to be a good student."

Her reaction was playful, not coy, and she was totally unaware of the rush of desire her words and tone awoke in Rick.

He held her tightly, his eyes closed, and then he slowly drew his hands down her back and circled her waist. Reluctantly he pushed her away. "Time for dinner. Shall we go down to the restaurant or—"

"Oh, let's just order something up, Rick. That way we can cuddle and nibble and talk. It'll be fun."

"Oh, yeah." He swallowed hard, already planning a cold shower for dessert!

They ordered club sandwiches and chips and cold beer from room service, and sat on the bed, leaning against the headboard and dropping crumbs on the sheets and laughing at Laurie's foam moustache. When the sandwiches were gone, they split another beer, drinking from the same can, putting their mouths on the same place, smiling at each other over the rim.

"This is wonderful!" She grinned, licking the foam off her lips with her tongue. "Here, you've got some too." Without thinking she leaned over and sipped the foam from his mouth.

Rick stiffened in surprise, then caught her around the waist and swung her up on top of his lap so that her knees spanned his thighs and her body was trapped against his. Holding her tightly with one hand, he pushed the empty plates over the edge of the bed with the other. Then he grinned back at her. "Try that again, woman. Now I'm ready for you!"

"Now I'm not," she answered, breathless.

"Then I'll go slow." He kissed her neck and the tender hollow at the base of her throat, and slipped one finger beneath the neckline of her sweater and dusted kisses across her pale, translucent skin.

"How about taking off a little of this clothing?" he whispered, his warm breath causing shivers across her breasts.

Laurie felt her nipples swell and harden, her whole body begin to ache.

"How about if you go first?" she asked quickly, pressing one hand flat against her chest.

"All right." Leaning back, watching her, he tugged his shirt free of his slacks, grabbed hold of the bottom edge and pulled it quickly up over his chest and off.

A sharp stab of desire pierced Laurie.

She reached out and pressed both hands flat against his skin, feeling his springy dark hair beneath her palms. Her hands looked small and narrow against his chest, and even when she spread her fingers, she could barely span its width. As her pinkies brushed against his nipples they hardened, and Laurie's eyes jumped to his face in surprise. "Oh, I'm sorry! Oh, Rick, I—"

"No, no, sweet thing. Don't be wasting one tiny breath on being sorry." His voice was husky with desire. "Don't be scared of my body. It's just goin' slightly crazy being this close to you."

"But it's okay, isn't it? I mean, I feel so wonderful all of a sudden. So happy and free. You'd tell me if I was out of line, wouldn't you? If I was doing something you didn't like—"

"Oh, I like it, all right. That's not the problem."

"Well, to be honest," she answered, laughter bubbling in her throat, "I like it too!"

"Come here." He slid his body down flat onto the bed and drew her beside him, his hands moving slowly from her shoulders to her hips, molding her body to the length of his. "There, see how nicely everything fits?" His hands stroked her shoulders and back, tracing the ridge of her spine through the soft knit of her sweater. Her skirt had ridden up above her knees, and her legs were tucked between his. His hands found the small of her back, slid down, and moved softly over her buttocks, her skirt sliding against the silk of her panties. "Lovely . . . your body is so lovely."

"I . . . I didn't know. I—"

"You what?" He laughed, nipping her sharply on

the shoulder in sheer delight. "Darlin', you'll drive me crazy, I know it!"

Squirming against him, Laurie struggled to roll over onto the safe surface of the bed. "I think we're both a little crazy, Westin. And I think I'd better get off you or I'm going to be in trouble."

"I'm in trouble already!" he whispered as he nuzzled her ear playfully.

"Rick, really, I . . . I need to breathe. You know, air. Oxygen. Let's calm down and talk."

Flinging one arm up over his eyes, he drew a deep, steadying breath. "Let me count to a hundred a couple of times, and we can start a conversation."

"Did I do something wrong?"

"No," he answered quickly, lowering his arm and grinning at her. His eyes were smoke-dark, with fire sparking in their depths. "Nope, *you* are perfect. It's my imperfect self-control that's giving me a hard time. But"—he laughed, his teeth flashing white in the darkness—"I have a feeling I'm going to get plenty of practice."

With a smile Laurie slipped from the bed and snapped on the light. "I may as well get ready for bed. I'll just have to wear my slip," she said, and disappeared into the bathroom.

Rick let his imagination run wild as he got out of his slacks and slid under the covers. Silk and lace. Sheer, with a plunging neckline and thin straps that he'd slip with agonizing slowness off her shoulders—

The door opened and Laurie stepped out in a shapeless white cotton slip salvaged from the convent.

"Hi." She looked at him from under her lashes, feeling the heat climb steadily over the slip's modest neckline, wishing she had something else to wear, something lacy and pretty and feminine. "I

. . . I didn't expect anyone to see me," she began haltingly, then was overcome with shyness.

"It's fine, Laurie. You look like Juliet, or Sleeping Beauty. Come over here." His voice downshifted into sexy. "Let the prince give you your kiss!"

And it was all right. She felt pretty again, desirable and desiring. She sauntered over to the bed, leaned down, and offered him her lips.

He took all of her, pulling her back into bed and tumbling them both around like puppies.

"Whoa! Halt! Uncle!" She giggled, disentangling herself from his arms and legs. "Don't you think we'd better get some sleep? You have a show tomorrow, remember?"

"No problem, sweet thing. You're the only thing I've got to concentrate on."

She curled up next to him, studying him with great seriousness. After a moment she smiled and tucked her hand beneath her cheek, her wide eyes still resting on his face. "Rick Westin, you are a very handsome man, maybe the handsomest man in the whole world. And very sexy!"

He gave a sharp yelp of laughter. "Thank you, ma'am. Is that your opinion after years of research?"

"After years of dreaming. That counts!"

"Yes, it does. I'll bow to your judgment."

"Wise decision. Now, tell me, am I allowed to do this?" She kissed his mouth sweetly, a light butterfly touch.

"Yes . . . that's fine."

"And this?" She drew her hand slowly over his shoulders, enjoying the invisible curve of the muscle beneath the warm smoothness of his skin.

"Yes . . ."

"And this?" She bent her head and placed her lips where her hand had been, where the bunched muscles of his shoulder smoothed into the flat plane of his chest.

She felt him jump, heard the hiss of his indrawn breath. "Now we're in trouble again!"

"Oops!"

Heated laughter rumbled in his throat. "Go to sleep, woman, before I forget my promise and I *do* attack you. Sleep! Now!"

Obediently she turned on her side, her back to him, and he nestled against her, one arm wrapped possessively around her waist.

"Good night, Banjo Man."

"Good night, darlin'."

"You know," she whispered, "I think you're going to be an easy man to fall in love with."

"Only for you," he said, thinking his chest was going to explode. "But now that's all that counts. And you, you're like a star so new in the night sky that no one's ever seen it shine before."

Laurie smiled to herself, balanced her body against his, and slipped into sleep.

Rick Westin was awake all night, but he didn't mind.

Eight

Rick had trouble getting dressed in the morning.

Laurie was bursting with new emotions, and longed to try them all out. How wonderful to feel her skin tingle, her mouth go dry, her insides melt, her nipples tighten. Pulse, respiration, temperature—everything was fantastically abnormal!

She walked her fingers down his spine as he slid from bed to answer the wake-up call. She rubbed her cheek against his bare back as he shaved. She tugged playfully at the hair on his chest as he disappeared into his clothes.

"Now, cut it out!" he'd order with a laugh, not meaning it, and take her in his arms for another kiss.

She didn't taste breakfast, and he shrugged and ate her toast and blushed when he met her adoring, wide-eyed gaze.

"Hey! Cut it out, now," he repeated, then gave up and leaned across the table to kiss her again.

It was without a doubt the craziest experience of

Rick Westin's life: spending a sleepless night with the woman of his dreams, fighting the painful tug of physical need, wanting her more than he'd ever wanted anything in his life, and having Laurie awaken with the incredible aura of a woman fulfilled . . . simply by having spent the night beside him. Maybe they taught something in those convents he ought to find out about!

The concert was scheduled for one o'clock, and by noon the auditorium at the University of Pennsylvania was jammed. Rick introduced her to the other performers. The names were all unfamiliar to her, although they elicited their share of screams from the waiting crowd.

"Do you want to watch from backstage?" he asked. "It'll be a lot less crowded."

"Nope! I'm going to be right out front, in the middle of all those people. I want to see you the way they do—a stranger, a sexy banjo player with wild black hair and inscrutable eyes, and I'll listen to you sing and indulge my fantasies. . . ."

"Write 'em down and I'll work on them tonight!"

Laurie had never been to a large concert before, certainly not during her five years in the convent, and before that, in high school, her father had forbidden it. Now, having edged her way into the thick of things, she was overwhelmed by the noise, the press of bodies, the jostling and stamping and shouting. And when Rick came onstage he did seem a stranger, and oddly powerful. The crowd hushed, as if his playing tamed them. She watched them watching him, clapping their hands to his music, laughing at his jokes, shouting out requests.

It was a strange sensation. Part of her was the woman who had spent the night with him, and part was a shy young girl who stood lost among his other fans. Yet when it was over she was swept by an odd sense of elation. She alone could go back-stage and claim him.

Something of her feeling must have shown in her expression, because Rick took one look at her face and frowned.

"Come on, let's take a quick walk around campus. We've got an hour before our obligatory appearance at the president's cocktail party." He didn't wait for an answer, just slipped an arm around her waist and headed her away from the crowd.

"Rick"—she smiled up at him—"you were wonderful!"

"It was a good concert . . . good audience," he answered guardedly.

"No, I mean you. You were great! You should do that all the time; they loved you!"

"Laurie, sometimes you scare me." His brows were dark as thunder above his clouded eyes. "You're all or nothing, black or white. Life isn't that simple, darlin'. Not real life. Listen, those people don't love me. They see the flash and the perform-ance, but that's all. How many do you think really hear the stories, or picture the lives that make those songs? That's what *I* care about."

"But if you did more concerts, more people would hear."

"They don't listen, not most of them." He stopped and leaned against a tree, pulling her close. She stood with her feet between his, her arms around his neck, looking up at him.

"It's just so exciting!"

"Only at first, Laurie," he insisted, his voice rough-edged. "But not for long. And it's all on the surface. Too many people are trying to score, and they all want something, but not what you want to give."

"What *do* you want to give?"

"The music. The heritage. A glimpse at a world that's fast disappearing. But I don't want to give 'me.' That I only want to share . . . and only with one person."

She smiled, tipping her head back. "Me?"

"You." He nested his chin in the hollow of her neck and went on talking, almost to himself. "See, what I like is to play to a small audience, where I can see everyone's face, and know if I've made contact. That's why the Stage is good for me. That, and because it lets me get back into the hills every year."

Laurie stiffened. Her smile slipped. "Oh, I had forgotten about that."

"Well, it's not until April, but you'll love it!" He grinned, his dark eyes shining. "It's all so beautiful: the people, the countryside, the whole pace and texture of life."

"But . . . but you're gone for six months. On a motorcycle. I've never even ridden on one!"

"Hey, that's all right. I'll teach you to ride a 'cycle. You won't believe how great it is, moving across the fields and hills with the wind in your face, no car between you and the sounds and feel of the land. And we'll stop at farmhouses and little roadside stands, and talk to the people. Meet their kids and their old folks, and eat their cooking, and—"

"And my job! I do have a job, you know."

Rick narrowed his eyes. "You said yourself that it was just a filler. It's not a career . . . something you love."

"Maybe not, but I can't go off and do nothing for six months. I wasn't brought up that way!"

"I'm not telling you not to do anything. Maybe out there you'll find something you really *want* to do. I know that every year I think, 'Here's something else I wish I could do: paint, or write, or take photographs, or learn to whittle or weave or spin wool—' "

"That's because you're an incurable romantic! Pie in the sky! What if I want to do something sensible that I'm already good at, like teaching school?"

"Great! Then teach school, and we'll only hit the road when school's out. There's no problem."

"Oh, yes, there is!" she flung back, tossing her head. "I just can't think of what it is!"

She glowered at him, daring him to give in to the grin that lurked at the corners of his mouth.

And then she started to laugh, and the tension vanished like smoke. "What was that?" she asked, giggling against his shoulder.

"I don't know. I think I riled that Irish temper of yours. I'm going to have to learn to watch for storm signals!"

"Hurricane warnings!" she teased back, then sighed. Exhaustion was starting to set in, creeping up from her toes. "You're just a lot to handle all of a sudden."

"Too much too soon, darlin'?" he asked softly.

"Maybe," she whispered, hating to admit it, even to herself.

"Well, we'll take it slow. Do you want to keep the room and stay over again?"

"You call that taking it slow?" she asked with a gasp. "No, I want to have a good gulp of brandy at that cocktail party, pile into that speedy Jeep of yours, and sleep on Ellen's safe little couch for at least twenty-four hours straight!"

Rick gave her a sweet, lingering kiss, then bent his head and whispered into the silkiness of her hair, "All right, my darlin'. As my mother used to say, 'There are no shortcuts to heaven.' "

Nine

Laurie had felt dizzy and faint all morning, through the staff meeting, the briefings, the research.

"You work too hard, punkin'," Paula had cautioned kindly over sandwiches at lunch. "And you're still taking everything so seriously. Remember, laugh a little more, at yourself, at me, at some of the stuffed shirts who come in here claiming omniscience. Anybody. But ease up, Laurie."

The office gopher was certain it was the beginning of a new outbreak of Legionnaire's disease, and kept to the far side of the room. Senator Murphy decided she was getting the flu and should go home and rest or her father would have his hide.

There was no sense trying to explain that it was simply a case of growing pains. She didn't have the acne to go with it, so who would believe her?

Finally, drowning in well-intentioned advice, Laurie grabbed her blazer and fled the office in midday. She rode the bus along Massachusetts Avenue and tried to clear her mind, to sort out her feelings and pull everything back into some kind of perspective. But, after Philadelphia, it was like trying to rake leaves in the middle of a tornado.

Rick Westin was without a doubt the most wonderful thing that had ever happened to her, but her life suddenly felt like a roller-coaster ride. How in heaven's name was she supposed to know how to behave? Maybe there was a book she should read, a newspaper column, something!

"Miss?" the bus driver called over his shoulder. "Isn't this your stop?"

Laurie's head shot up, and her briefcase tumbled to the floor with a thud. "What? Oh, yes . . . thanks. I'm daydreaming again!" And she fled the bus and his amused stare.

After dropping her coat and case on a chair just inside the apartment door, Laurie headed for the kitchen. A cup of tea would revive her, she decided. Then maybe she'd straighten up the place and surprise Ellen. What was it the postulant mistress used to say? "An idle mind is the devil's workshop!"

She laughed wearily and leaned against the wall. The thrumming ache behind her eyebrows called for sleep, not tea, not dusting. And it might be an even better way to keep her mind off that banjo man, just until she could catch her breath.

Envisioning a quiet room and a cool bed, she hurried into the bedroom.

Later, Laurie couldn't be sure just what she'd noticed first: the fact that the room was very dark for the middle of the day, or the rustle of the sheets at her sudden entry, or the fact that the voice that sleepily asked, "Who's there?" was definitely not Ellen's! Perhaps it was all three at once that froze her to the spot while her eyes slowly adjusted to the dim light. There was Ellen, slowly awakening, lying right next to a man with tousled hair who leaned on one elbow and looked at her through half-closed eyes.

"Oh . . . oh. Oh, my," Laurie moaned through the icy fingers that she had instantly slapped over her mouth. Then, not pausing for another second, not giving her knees a single chance to play their silly game, she spun on her heel and fled the room.

Ellen followed a minute later, tying her bathrobe around her waist and then rubbing the sleep from her eyes.

"Ellen . . ." Laurie dropped down on the couch and stared, not trusting her voice, her hands hidden in her lap.

Ellen managed a contented half-smile. "Oh, it's all right, Laurie. I've been awakened before in the middle of a good dream." She walked over to the coffeepot and plugged it in. "I sure needed that sleep, though. Three nights on the graveyard shift in E.R. is enough to put hair on my chest."

"Ellen!" Laurie's strained voice bounced off the wall, her eyes darting back and forth from the bedroom door to Ellen.

Ellen looked up with a start and caught her glance. "Oh, Laurie, I'm sorry. I guess I'm too sleepy even to think straight. That's Dan—the resident I told you about, the one doing the rotation in Kansas City. Well, he's back, and everything's fine now between us. And he's dying to meet you."

Blissfully unaware of Laurie's reproving silence, Ellen poured herself a cup of steaming coffee and came to sit beside her friend. "But what about you, kiddo? What are you doing home in the middle of the day? Lose your job already?"

"Ellen!" Laurie's voice was harsh. "What is he doing in there?" Her accusing finger jabbed at the door.

Ellen's dreamy sense of contentment vanished.

Suddenly she realized that Laurie was not only shocked, she was angry.

Staring at Laurie, she lifted one eyebrow slowly. "Well, he's not taking a bath, that's for sure. Or playing tennis. He happens to be sleeping. He's been working day and night for ten solid weeks, just flew in, and he's exhausted." She threw the words at Laurie like darts. "I brought him home, fixed him a hot meal, and we went to bed. Together. Dan and I. We're in love, Laurie. And we *loved* each other." She watched Laurie closely to make sure the words were registering.

They were. Laurie's face turned quite pink. "But here, Ellen? Right here?"

"Would you have preferred we take a motel room?"

Perhaps if she hadn't been so tired, she would have handled it differently, but Ellen was losing her cool. "Laurie, I love you. And I know adjustments are hard—I had some problems coming out after just six *weeks*. But good grief, wake up and smell the coffee! Things are different now. You're not eighteen. You're a woman. *I'm* a woman!"

Laurie shook her head and ran a hand through her hair. "But Ellen, you shouldn't be—"

"What? What shouldn't I be, Laurie? Shouldn't be in love? Dammit, I am fully capable of being responsible for my actions. I don't need you to try to be responsible for them too. You're going to have your hands full just taking care of Laurie O'Neill!"

Laurie began to protest, but Ellen wasn't finished. "You know, I wonder if it's really me you're judging or if you're so mixed up about your own emotions that you're condemning me because *you* feel guilty!"

Laurie sat still, Ellen's words hitting home with the sureness of truth. She felt the hot burn of tears on her cheeks. "Oh, Ellen, I'm so sorry. After all you've done—"

In a second Ellen was beside her, her arms around Laurie's shaking shoulders. Her voice was soft and soothing. "It's all right, Laurie. It's okay. I know it's hard to sort it all out."

Laurie brushed away the tears with the back of her hand. "Maybe if I hadn't met Rick so soon, if I just could have taken one thing at a time, it would be different. But now . . . now I want him so much, and I'm so confused!" She forced a laugh. "It was so much easier back in Father Leo's moral theology class, wasn't it? All the rules were there in that fat little book: what you do and what you don't do."

Ellen laughed aloud at the memory of the elderly Franciscan priest who had lectured morals to them *ad infinitum* during their postulancy. "Remember this one—'how far can you keep on doing what you're doing before it becomes a don't?' "

"And 'when tacit agreement becomes just as bad as the real thing'!" Laurie was laughing out loud now too. "Remember that crazy song we made up to remember who could marry whom and when?"

A flood of hilarious memories engulfed the two women, and the tension between them was broken.

Laurie smiled softly. "You know, there was something nice and neat and secure about that little book, though, having everything there in black and white. It's too bad life isn't like that, isn't it?"

Ellen heard the panic creep back into Laurie's voice, and nodded sympathetically.

"Well, I suppose it's more complicated this way, honey. But as for me, I'm not much of a black-and-white person. I find that adding color to life makes it a lot more interesting. There's a lot to be said for taking responsibility for your own actions, and using the good sense God gave you to figure out what to do with your life."

Laurie stood and walked over to the window. "Yes, I guess you're right."

She drew her finger along the sill and rubbed the dust absentmindedly between thumb and fingertips. Her thoughts had sped elsewhere—to Rick. One thing was sure: Rick Westin would never fit into a neat, boring, black-and-white life. And that wasn't what *she* wanted either. So the first thing on the agenda, even before she could figure out her love life, was to figure out who the heck she was!

Biting her lip and mustering her courage, she took the first step.

"Ellen, I'm moving out."

"What?" Ellen jumped up. "No, Laurie, you don't have to do that. Just because—"

"Just because I need to stand on my own two feet, that's why!" She grinned and glanced at the closed bedroom door. "It's not because of today, honest. At least not in the way you think. Ellen, when I needed you these past weeks to keep me from drowning in this big city, you were here, and you've been great! But I think I have to learn how to swim by myself, and the tide is right!"

"Are you sure about this? You don't usually make such snap decisions."

"Didn't. This is the new me!" Laurie's eyes sparkled. "And you can't tell me it won't be nice to brush your teeth without having to do it over someone's shoulder, and to be able to open your closet door without first moving a suitcase and three shoe boxes."

Ellen laughed. "I guess we have been a little cramped, but I haven't minded, Laurie. I really haven't!"

"I know you haven't. That's what makes you such a special friend. And I hope you won't mind when I come pounding on your door when I get lonesome." She glanced at Dan's jacket lying across the back of the couch and laughed. "On second thought, maybe I'll call first."

Ten

Rick loved the idea of her moving out on Ellen . . . and in with him!

He met her right after work Tuesday afternoon, and took her straight to his place.

"No, Rick," Laurie said, standing in the doorway, her fists pressed firmly against her waist. "No, you don't understand at all."

"But it'd be perfect, darlin'." Rick grabbed her hand and drew her into a warm, sun-drenched living room. "Look, just look at all this room! And there're bedrooms all over the place, a kitchen big enough for cookin' haute cuisine or Texas chili or collard greens—or all of 'em at the same time!"

Laurie had barely had time to enjoy the wonderful look of his solid oak furniture and the mountain crafts that were everywhere in the room—the spinning wheel at the hearth, the wooden carvings of an old man and woman standing proudly beside the window, a dulcimer and old banjo hanging on the muted wallpaper next to a colorful Appalachian quilt—before Rick was dragging her to the back of the narrow Georgetown town house.

He pointed enthusiastically through the kitchen windows to a small brick patio, completely surrounded by flower beds and neatly trimmed bushes. A wide rope hammock swung lazily from two trees, and a large mutt reclined beneath it. "See? It's perfect! Man's best friend. A place to lie your tired body down after a long day and let the senate dust blow away. A place to bring out a banjo and sing with the birds. A place to—"

"Rick, *no.*" Laurie reached one hand up to stop the flow of words.

"Wait, Laurie. Look at this!" And he drew her up a narrow flight of stairs, polished and smooth and covered with a fine old runner. Four rooms fanned out from the small hallway upstairs. "See? Just like I said. Why, we could put your things in here." A lovely old four-poster bed met her gaze as he pulled her into the doorway. "We could move that bigger dresser in if you wanted or—"

"Stop it!" Laurie's laughter softened her words. Her eyes swept from the bed to Rick's tall, wonderful body, and she mustered up all the strength she could find buried beneath her burgeoning emotions.

"Rick Westin, this is silly, and you know it. I've got to find my own place."

A frown tugged at the corners of his mouth, and he stepped back, pouting like a disappointed child. "Hm-m-m, you're determined, aren't you?"

Laurie slipped her hands into the pockets of her pants. "Yep, I am, Banjo Man. And a lot of that determination I owe to you, for helping me feel so strong and good about myself." She leaned against the smooth, worn bedpost. "It'd be so easy to fall back into having someone else make the decisions for me, care for me. But I can't—I won't. I thought you'd be proud of me."

He was . . . proud *and* excited by the new fire in her eyes these days.

"Okay, darlin'. You win. But on one condition."

Laurie narrowed her eyes suspiciously.

"That you at least let me help you move—and make sure the lock on your door is a strong one!"

After two weeks of looking, the only apartment Laurie was able to find was on the fourth floor of an older building not far from the hospital where Ellen worked. A nurse friend was leaving town and wanted someone to finish out the lease. Ellen had begrudgingly arranged for Laurie to take over as soon as possible, listening halfheartedly to Laurie's insistence that she needed to be alone.

Alone. She hadn't been alone since . . . since never, that was when. The thought at once terrified and intrigued her. And she had signed the lease in a moment of awful surrender to the future.

One load was all it took in Rick's sturdy Jeep to move her belongings: two suitcases—she had bought herself a number of new clothes—and a few stray pieces of kitchenware Ellen had insisted she take along.

"You did say it was furnished, right, babe?" Rick asked as they struggled up the stairs with an assortment of boxes and a wild array of plants Rick had picked up at the farmers' market.

"Sparsely," Laurie admitted, nibbling nervously on her lower lip. Then her face brightened, and she added quickly, "But that's fine. I don't need clutter. Just a bed, a few chairs. You know, the essentials." She'd lived with much less for years; whatever was there would be fine.

"Well, darlin'"—Rick kicked open the door to

number 205 with the toe of his boot and took a cursory glance around—"that's what you got . . . the bare essentials!"

They stood together in the doorway and surveyed the tiny room. A well-polished hardwood floor reflected the shape of a patterned hide-a-bed and two chairs. Off to one side was a round oak table and chairs, and beyond that, on the other side of a divider, a tiny kitchen.

Laurie stood silently for several moments, her head reeling with memories and sensations of times past. Slowly she took in the sunlit windows, the high ceilings, the old wooden molding edging the walls . . . the stuff of her new home.

Rick was quiet beside her, one arm resting lightly around her shoulder, ready to sweep her away from it all should she but say the word. Beneath her thin cotton blouse he could feel her tremble, but he found her silence impossible to read.

"Well, darlin'?" he asked at last.

Laurie tilted her head back and met his eyes. She knew what he was thinking: that this was an awful place, small and empty and cold. How could she explain to him what it meant to her? That this tiny stark apartment meant for the first time in a lifetime she could come and go as she pleased, that she could eat what she wanted, put her bed in the middle of the room if she wanted, and dance around it at three in the morning if she wanted! Her eyes crinkled at the corners and a lovely smile lit her face. "Oh, Rick, it's beautiful."

Rick held his silence, watching her with a bemused smile as she walked slowly into the room, her head held high and her face aglow with wonder.

"It's mine . . . my apartment. My own apartment."

She ran her hands slowly over the oak tabletop,

then walked over to the couch, then back to the kitchen, her tempo increasing with each step. "Rick, it's going to be perfect—just perfect!" She raced to the windows. "We can put some of your plants here—and if I get a little rug for over there . . ." She spun around, her arms flying through the air and sending tiny dust flecks dancing in the sunlight. "It's absolutely grand!"

Rick caught her on the second spin and pulled her close, his eyes shining brightly. "Laurie O'Neill, you are something else. Each day you're something else! What will tomorrow bring to my wild Irish rose?"

She welcomed the kiss that slowly formed between them, the soft crush of his lips upon her own as he held her gently and pressed her into the warmth of his body. There was no fear left, for the feel of Rick's body against her own was becoming as natural and welcome as sunlight.

Wrapping her arms around his neck, she kissed him back, eagerly, passionately. "You know, Rick," she murmured, "I used to worry about whether I'd know how to do that right—about whether I'd get my lips in the right place, whose went where. It doesn't matter if teenagers flub it up, but a woman my age should know about such things, and I wasn't sure I did!"

"Well, darlin'," Rick said huskily, "you've been doing just fine! But if I, ah, don't put some fresh air between us soon, I'm afraid we're not going to . . . to get this place in working order."

Reluctantly, and with great effort, Rick settled his hands firmly on her shoulders and stepped back, taking in a lungful of air. "Now, Laurie, we need to make some sense out of this room."

Laurie watched him with emotions that swirled crazily through her body.

He confused her sometimes, stopping short

when she wanted nothing more than to press her body harder and harder against his and have him hold her there tightly. She craved all this cuddling and touching and kissing. Rick was like some exotic new food that awakened taste buds never used before, and she couldn't get enough of him. And though he came to her eagerly, and never forced the issue of their sleeping together, he often pushed her away suddenly, inexplicably. Laurie was too shy to ask, but she sensed that pushing her away was something Rick Westin did out of necessity, not choice.

Shaking her coppery hair to clear her head, she glanced around the room. "Well, Rick, there aren't a whole lot of choices."

"Of course there are!" He flopped down on the hide-a-bed and surveyed the room with exaggerated concentration. "Now, first, what kind of decor would interest you, madame?" He lifted one thick brow and tilted his head.

Laurie laughed. "Oh, early attic, I should think."

"Marvelous choice! And I know just the way to do it!" Rick leaped off the couch. "Of course! It's a terrific idea!"

Laurie stepped back curiously. "Oh?"

"A housewarming! That's what this place needs."

"A housewarming?" Wandering into the tiny strip of a kitchen, Laurie mulled over the idea.

"Sure," Rick insisted, his dark eyes flashing. "Next best thing to a house-raising!" He leaned his long frame against the chipped edge of the sink and rubbed a silken strand of her hair between two fingers. "You know, I helped out with one of those things a few years back when I was traveling through Tennessee, and it was great. Everyone came—uncles, aunts, cousins, friends. There was this old guy helping who was ninety if he was a day, and he didn't stop for a breath until the job was done. In *one* day we raised the walls of that house—it was somethin'! And passersby cheered us on as if we had just invented the wheel."

"Did you know the people?"

"Not when I came. Sure did when I left."

"You're such a strange man, Rick Westin." Laurie sighed, slipping down onto one of the oak chairs near the table.

"I'm not sure that's a compliment." Rick cocked his head to one side and grinned. "What kind of strange?"

"Well, first there's your life on the road, living with those people, never meeting a stranger, sleeping wherever and whenever—like a cowboy or a gypsy."

"Yeah, I'm sorta like that."

"And then here in Washington you've got this beautiful old Georgetown town house that my coworkers say is like gold to come by. I mean, you're a well-known entertainer, who probably . . . well, not that it's any of my business."

"What . . . makes a lot of money?" he prompted, amused by her sudden formality. This must be another of the many things one did not talk about in the convent.

"Well, yes, I guess." She looked up shyly.

"It's what I was trying to explain the other day, darlin'. I love my home here, *and* I love my traveling home out there. Sure, they're as different as ice cream and molasses, but both are sweet to my taste. See?"

"I think so."

"The fact is, I don't think of it as strange. I think it's more the way life ought to be. A balance. Does that make any sense, Laurie?"

Laurie nodded, a soft smile playing over her lips. "Sure. It makes lots of sense, Rick." She touched his arm lightly and her voice turned thoughtful. "A delicate balance. I think that's what I was missing in the convent. I tried to find it, but it never felt quite right. Somehow I wasn't able to hang on to Laurie O'Neill in the middle of everything else. I lost her, and became someone else."

Rick was leaning forward, watching her with dark intensity, wondering about that life, the years that were part of Laurie's past. She didn't talk easily about it, so he salvaged bits and pieces that she threw out at random, and patiently hoped that someday they'd form a picture he could understand.

Laurie felt the heat of his gaze and blushed. Wiping an imaginary crumb off the table, she tossed her head back and changed the subject. "Back to this housewarming, Westin. Just what do you have in mind?"

Rick accepted her mood swing, and began pacing around the room as if measuring space. "It'll be great! We'll be a little crowded, but that's okay—that's what makes it a house*warming*, after all. Simple and easy. We'll just do it, that's all. What do you say about Friday night, right after the show?"

"A housewarming Friday night? That's too soon. We've got to plan it!"

Rick waved away her objections. "What's to plan? I'll take care of the food and libations. You take care of opening the door when the guests arrive."

Suddenly Laurie threw her hands in the air, her eyes round. "Oh, Rick—we can't!"

"We can't?"

"No, we can't. For one very basic, very good reason. Except for you, Paula, Ellen, and Dan, I don't have any friends to invite!"

Rick's husky laughter swallowed her mournful protest. "Then, my sweet thing, we shall find you some friends! No problem at all. Why, I'll just go up and down the halls and—"

"Rick, stop it! I'm serious. Who would I invite?"

"You invite Paula, Ellen, and Dan. And I'll invite all my friends who have been badgering me for weeks to let them meet you. You see, Laurie"—he wound an arm around her waist and ran a finger slowly over the alluring curve of her cheek bone— "I've been very selfish. I've been keeping you all to myself. But I can't do that forever, much as I'd like to!"

"This will never work!" Laurie stared into the refrigerator. Plates of cheese and sausage and pungent antipasto glared silently back at her.

"It won't, you know. I'm not ready to meet Rick's friends. I don't *want* to meet them. What if they don't like me? What if I don't like them? And what in heaven's name will I say to a houseful of guests—*my* guests—whom I've never met?" She stabbed an innocent olive and shoved it into her mouth.

"I have the same trouble with those darn things—they never talk back." Ellen's laughing voice filtered into the kitchen from the doorway.

"Ellen!" Laurie spun around. "I didn't hear you!"

"That's because you were having an animated conversation with an olive." She grinned as she dropped a sackful of food on the table. "Laurie O'Neill, considering it's a dump, I think you've done wonderful things in here!" Her eyes flew around the apartment appreciatively.

Laurie had spent her whole week's salary on the apartment, but it had been worth it. Colorful throws brightened the drab furniture, and the flickering light of dozens of tiny candles grouped on the chipped mantel softened the bare ivory walls. At a flea market on Wisconsin Avenue she'd even found some huge, plump floor pillows that transformed the shadowy corners of the room into warm, inviting niches.

Laurie beamed her thanks. "Well, I hope there'll be enough room. Rick didn't say how many people he'd invited."

Frowning, she fidgeted with a pleat at the waist of her full cotton skirt. "I can't imagine anyone coming on such short notice, anyway. This was really a silly idea. A *dumb* idea. Stupid!" She tried to force a little nonchalance into her voice. "You know, my partying experience leaves a little to be desired. I'm used to a good, heated game of volley-ball followed by fruit juice and cookies in the community room!"

Ellen laughed as she began pulling chips, egg rolls, and nacho sauce out of her brown sack. "You're wrong, Laurie. It was a great idea! I've met a few of Rick's friends, and they're very nice. They'll love you—just like Dan did once he found out you weren't a ghost who prowls around bedrooms—"

"—sprinkling holy water!" Laurie laughed at the memory of her first meeting with Dan. When he had finally tumbled out of bed that day, Laurie had found in Ellen's boyfriend a warm and witty friend. He was good for Ellen, Laurie had decided, and she almost envied the open and comfortable flow of affection between them. It seemed so much simpler, somehow, than her heated passion for Rick.

"Well," Laurie said with a groan, "I guess there's no turning back now, is there? But I sure wish Rick would get here! He dropped off all this food right after the show, then disappeared again."

"Well, he's back, and he's not alone!" Ellen announced a second before his enthusiastic pounding nearly broke down the door.

"Open, sesame!" Rick called in a deep voice that

caused doors to open all down the hall. "Company's here!"

The first two hours were a blur to Laurie. She plastered a smile on her face and did all she could to be the gracious hostess. Rick's friends continued to arrive, filling the tiny studio apartment with their laughter and animated conversation . . . and surprise gifts that stunned her. Plants and towels and place mats followed a lovely old coffee table which the producer of Rick's show didn't want anymore. The set designer brought a wonderful painting of old Georgetown. There were end tables, lovely handmade pots, more plants, and enough kitchen gadgets to open a store. No one came empty-handed, and Laurie was in awe of how quickly they helped turn her apartment into a home.

A tall, thin woman with short, curly hair settled down next to Laurie, folding her blue-jean clad legs into a pretzel. "You've been a mystery to us, Laurie. We've all been speculating when Rick was going to bring you out of the woodwork."

The words were beginning to sound like an irritating echo; nearly every one of Rick's friends had said the same thing! A gnawing, painful thought began to grow in Laurie's mind. Perhaps *he* had been afraid she wouldn't fit in. Afraid they'd wonder about his sanity, now that he was spending so much time on someone as . . . as uncolorful as Laurie O'Neill. And the saddest part of all was that she *didn't* fit in.

"Rick said you're a teacher?" Hans Hanson, the bearded producer, turned from an animated discussion on the effect of politics on the arts and joined the conversation.

"Yes, I taught school. In Pennsylvania." Unable to think of anything that would add sparkle to that topic, Laurie continued, "I also worked in Pittsburgh's inner city on Saturdays, teaching in a Head Start program."

That piece of information was greeted with nods and smiles, but since the whole program had dissolved from lack of funding, she again ran out of words.

All around her Laurie heard tidbits of wonderful talk: people interested in obscure poets, people active in social causes, people discussing speeches and plays and recording artists she had never heard of. And each time Laurie pushed herself into a group, the talk slowly died as they turned their attention to her, seeking to know her better, to discover the charm that had captivated Rick Westin. And each time, Laurie fell into silence after two short, simple sentences.

Escaping into the tiny kitchen, she buried her head in the refrigerator and agonized over her next course of action.

Darn it, she felt as out of place in there as a penguin in Miami. But it was *her* apartment. She wasn't going to be a stranger here. No! she fumed at herself. Laurie O'Neill, stand up and fight. Make yourself a part of things if it kills you! *Be* someone!

Mustering up all the courage she could find, then reinforcing it with the unfamiliar taste of a huge swig of wine, she attacked the party with a vengeance.

She spotted her first target. There was Raj, an Indian historian at the Smithsonian Institution who spoke in such lofty terms no one seemed to understand him, deep in conversation with Helene, a curvaceous actress with a cloud of blond hair. Laurie squeezed in between the two and smiled brightly.

Raj nodded pleasantly and offered her a taste of the Indian liquor he had brought. Flushed, she took the tiny glass, offered a toast and swallowed the contents in a single gulp.

Raj stared. Helene looked on in awe. And Laurie's eyes shot open in pained surprise. The burning sensation in her throat traveled quickly to the pit of her stomach, then shot into every single available inch of her body. Gasping for air, she took the glass of water Helene thrust into her hand and poured it down her throat.

"Wow!" She wiped the moisture from her forehead and upper lip and smiled appreciatively. "Thank you, Raj, that was interesting. Certainly not your ordinary table wine," she joked, "but a real treat for the taste buds!"

The story would be told many times thereafter, each time becoming a bit more dramatic, until future friends would hear about the night Laurie O'Neill single-handedly drank a jug of Raj's strongest, most potent Indian brew—and lived to tell about it.

"Whew!" Raj stroked his beard and looked at Laurie with new admiration. "You are quite a powerful drinker, Laurie O'Neill. Even the tribes I've visited did not down their liquor quite that aggressively."

The fire in her stomach had now subsided into a lovely warmth, and Laurie felt fine. Absolutely fine! A little light-headed, perhaps, but quite relaxed and in the swing of things—at last!

She slipped out of her shoes and plopped down on one of the huge pillows. "Come on down, the weather's fine!" She giggled, her face flushed and her eyes shining happily. "Now, Raj, I want to know all about your work. And yours, too, Helene. Rick has told me so much about you both."

"Unfair." Helene laughed just as several others joined the lively group. "You know about us, but he's told us nothing about you, Laurie."

The group noisily agreed, and Laurie suddenly wanted to draw them all into her confidence. They were such wonderful people! And, dammit, if Rick wouldn't tell them about Laurie O'Neill, *she* would!

"Well," she started, wondering vaguely why her voice was echoing around her head; it felt like a halo, she thought, giggling at the image. "Well, there's really quite a lot to tell, folks. Right now I'm working for Senator Murphy, up on the Hill."

Several voices immediately chimed into the conversation, talking about the senator and his work with various committees.

"Yes," Laurie broke in, not yet finished or ready to be upstaged, "and for five years before that I was a Sister."

She settled back on her folded legs and smiled sweetly, so pleased with her active part in the conversation and the warmth flowing through her that she failed to notice the stunned silence that had fallen on the entire group.

Finally she looked around and registered their total noncomprehension.

An intent frown wrinkled her smooth forehead. "A Sister. You know, a nun. A bride of the Church." She slid her hand over her forehead to cover her hair and sat up very straight, her face melting into a pious, madonnalike expression. "You know, like this." She smiled again and looked over at Helene. "It was actually a very fascinating career—for a while. Certainly nothing like acting, but interesting just the same."

Out of the corner of her eye she could see Rick standing behind Raj, a surprised smile on his face. She winked at him, then looked back at Helene.

Helene's mouth snapped open and shut, then open again. "You were a . . . with a hab—in the conv—"

"Yes." And Laurie launched into an animated,

detailed, blow-by-blow account of how her hair was cut, when she began wearing the habit, how she managed to keep the vows of poverty, chastity, and obedience . . . and what happened to feminine pride when she had to cook bacon for two hundred and fifty people, dressed in heavy serge and a veil. "The smell was there for *weeks*, pressed into that veil like bubble gum! To this day I have a tough time being friends with pigs!"

She didn't even notice that the whole room was listening now, everyone's stunned reserve at her surprise announcement shattered into crazy laughter by the anecdotes she related with relish.

Soon they were peppering her with questions about rules and mysterious elements of the curious life that none of them knew anything about. Laurie gulped down the hot coffee Ellen set before her, laughed and talked and shared experiences with the roomful of people until the candles were burned to their bases, the last bit of food was swallowed up, and the silvery sliver of moonlight coming through the curtainless windows caught yawns and sprawling bodies in its pathway.

Leaning into Rick's side, she thanked her new friends for coming and finally, through muffled yawns, managed to convince Ellen and Dan that she and Rick could manage the clean-up shift by themselves.

Rick flicked off the overhead light and led her over to the pile of pillows on the floor. Pulling her down with him into the cushiony softness, he let out a long, exaggerated sigh that rustled the new stillness in the room.

"Whew! What a housewarming." He traced a single moonbeam over Laurie's cheeks before he slipped his arm around her back and pulled her close into the heated hollow his body had made in the cushions. "Promise me one thing, sweet thing." Pleased laughter laced his deep voice. "Promise me you'll never audition for my job!"

Laurie pressed closer, absorbing his delicious warmth. Her head was clear of the foggy feeling that had taken over a while back, and was filled now with a dizzying pleasure—the pleasure of having fun, of sharing, of being honest about who she was and what she'd done with her life so far.

" 'Fraid I'll upstage you, Banjo Man?" she teased, tucking her head under his chin and kissing the hollow of his throat.

Rick let his head fall back against the wall and looked at her from under his half-closed lids. "Laurie, remember when I said I was going to prove I was wonderful offstage as well as on? Well, I think tonight's the night."

Eleven

An eager desire flickered in Rick's dark eyes.

Laurie froze. It had been just a heartbeat since she had nuzzled under his chin for that kiss, and her hands still rested on his shoulders, her lips on his throat. But in that tiny slice of time she had felt his body change. His muscles had stretched and tensed, as if, after being restricted too long, they had been set free.

She gulped, and tried to pull away. If she could look him in the eye and make some joke, tease him, tickle him, maybe she could get things back under control.

But he held her tightly against him, not moving, just binding her to him by the hard strength of his hands on her back.

"Don't run away, darlin'."

His breath slid over the crown of her head and down her spine, waking shivers all along her body.

"Rick? Rick, I think I could use a sip of something."

"No. All you need is me."

"How do you know that?" she whispered, tipping her head back, her mouth close to his ear.

"Because all I need is you."

"Is that why your heart is beating so hard?"

"Yes, that's why. And yours?" He didn't wait for an answer, but curved one hand around her ribs and pressed his palm under the fullness of her breast.

She began to shake. Excitement was fizzing through her body like the bubbles in champagne. She was hot and trembly, ice-cold, and scared all at once.

His hand was so warm, so broad; it gave her something to measure her body by. All of a sudden she liked the size of her breasts, because there was just that perfect curve beneath them for his hand. The fragile arc of her rib cage lent itself to the shape of his palm; her waist was inches wider than his hand, and her belly button just a hand-span away. And both his hands, placed thumb to thumb, could probably cover her hips, circle her thigh, stretch along her thigh from knee to . . . to . . . oh, what should she call that hot, liquid center of her body?

Suddenly it didn't matter; her body was not waiting to be named! It was going on without her!

Little flames ran up her legs and over her belly. Her skin was tingling, feverish, and damp with arousal. Her pulse fluttered in her throat.

"I can feel your heart pounding," he whispered.

"Oh, heavens, I can feel a lot more than that!" she gasped, her voice all aquiver.

"Easy . . . easy, darlin'." He laughed softly. "We'll take it slow and easy."

"What if I can't?" She gulped, flinging her arms around his neck and pressing her face against his chest. "Oh, Rick, I love you; I want to make love with you. But I'm so dumb about all this. What if I do it wrong? What if I don't know how to do it at all?"

Laughing, he squeezed his eyes shut and buried his face in her hair. "Oh, my sweet darlin', this isn't a test. All you've got to do is love me, though it can't be half as much as I love you. The rest . . . well, the rest is easy. It's all wonder and magic. It's fantastic! It's riding to the moon, baby, just you and me. Here, you just have to relax."

"But I can't!" Her words were muffled against his shirt front.

The groan torn from his throat was half laugh, half curse. Then a knowing grin tugged at his lips. "Okay, then I'll play you a little song, darlin'."

With teasing sensuality he strummed his fingers across Laurie's back, his husky voice accompanying his pretend banjo playing:

> *Apples be ripe*
> *And nuts be brown,*
> *Petticoats up and*
> *Trousers down.*

"What kind of song is that?" she choked out, laughing, her face burning. "Rick Westin, you made that up!"

"No, it's an old folk ditty. Even the pioneers had fun sometimes!"

"But that's terrible!" She giggled, loving it.

"No, it's wonderful!"

"You're terrible!"

"No, *I'm* wonderful." His smile flashed with erotic excitement. "And *you're* wonderful. And we . . ." he said softly, timing his words to the movement of his hands as he unbuttoned her blouse, ". . . and we . . . are about . . . to make . . . wonderful love . . . together."

He peeled her blouse off her shoulders, bent his

head, and kissed the pale rise of her breast above her bra. His mouth was hot, his tongue rasping wetly across her flesh. She had never, never felt anything like it before! She wanted to close her eyes and float in the dark with nothing but this incredible feeling, but she couldn't take her eyes off him. She had to see as well as feel the thick brush of his dark hair against her ivory skin, the hard line of his jaw against the soft curve of her breast, the imprint of his mouth against her yielding flesh.

Washed by an unfamiliar yearning, she wriggled against him, trying to shrug free of her blouse. She managed to get one arm stuck in the sleeve.

"Help!" she gasped, breathless, and Rick grinned, tugged it off completely, and tore off his own shirt.

Grinning back, she wrapped her bare arms around his chest and was stunned by the flood of sensations that went through her. The tender skin of her breasts, the insides of her arms, the sensitive hollows beneath them, nothing had ever touched her in those places but the bland fabric of her own clothing. And here was the surprising heat of him, the texture of his skin and the electrifying brush of his dark, curly hair, the hardness of his muscle and the supple smoothness of his broad back. The heady musk of his scent filled her head, and she could taste him on her lips. Most incredible of all was the closeness, the unbelievable, dizzying closeness.

"Oh, Rick," she whispered, wanting to tell him everything she was feeling, finding no adequate words. It was all too new, too wonderful.

He understood without words and kissed her, crushing his lips against hers in a frenzy of passion.

His warm and tender hand stroked her body

from breast to belly and up and down the ridge of her spine. Then both hands settled at the waistband of her skirt, and he unfastened the button and slipped it down over her hips.

It all happened so fast she didn't think to protest, and then his hands were gliding over her thighs and hips, curving lovingly around her buttocks, and it was all more wonderful than she had ever imagined! She gave herself up to the feel of his hands on her body, and felt a new flame shooting and leaping through her. She was melting, melting beneath his touch.

And then he slipped his fingers beneath the band of her panties, and fear shot through her like an electric shock.

"Wait . . . wait, please," she said, gasping, and he stopped and cradled her in his arms, his breath torn to rags in his throat.

"It's all right, darlin'. I was going too fast, too fast."

"But it *is* wonderful," she protested, her eyes huge and pleading.

"That it is!" He laughed, making everything all right. "Hey, I forgot to give you your present." Rocking back on his heels, he crouched for a moment, head bent, his shoulders heaving, and then he looked up at her and flashed that heart-stopping grin of his. "Did you think I came to your party empty-handed?"

"I thought your heart was gift enough," she whispered.

The earth rocked beneath Rick's feet. He covered his eyes with one hand for a moment, then smiled at her, his dark eyes blazing.

Laurie's face was washed in the same glow of happiness. There was a moment of exquisite pleasure between them, and then Laurie said, "Well, sir, about this present you mentioned . . ."

He was gone for a second, then came back and knelt beside her. He held out a thin square box tied with a huge bow. "For you."

She unwrapped it, opened the white tissue, and gave a soft little cry of happiness. "Oh, it's beautiful, beautiful!"

It was a large silk scarf, shimmering with a rainbow of colors against a peacock-blue background. A look of delight lit her face as she lifted the silk square and rubbed her face against it. "Oh, I love it, Rick. Thank you!"

She stood, naked except for her bra and panties, and tied the scarf around her neck without a hint of shyness. The long ends fluttered against her bare skin, the colors catching the light in the candle-glow.

Rick smiled and got to his feet, watching her with pleasure. "Here, let's try this. . . ."

He untied the scarf and retied it first around her waist, its silken folds circling her in iridescent hues, then over her shoulders, then gypsy style around her hips, seemingly unaware of how his touch brushed fire against her bare skin. "Nice." He grinned, stepping back each time to admire his handiwork. "You certainly do something for that little piece of silk!"

"I'm glad. And now you can do something for me, Mr. Westin. Kiss me again."

He narrowed his eyes, studying her flushed face. "But you know what that will lead to, Ms. O'Neill," he whispered.

"I certainly hope so!" she answered.

He stepped close, cupped her lovely face in his hands, and kissed her.

With a quiver of pure delight, Laurie circled his back with her hands, tracing patterns on his warm skin. Sliding her palms down to the waistband of his slacks, she moved her hands around to his front.

She felt him tense, his kiss deepening, his body straining toward hers.

Pulling her lips away just a fraction of an inch, she whispered against his mouth, "May I?"

He groaned in response, a harsh sound of pure desire.

Giggling, her head spinning, she unsnapped the button. "Incredible!"

"You bet!" He laughed, and stepped back. "Okay, now the zipper."

"Oh, I can't!"

"Sure you can; here—" he directed, and, catching hold of her hand, he placed it against the front of his body and helped her guide the zipper down its track.

Laurie thought she was going to die! Faint! Melt away into a little puddle of excitement. She was shaking with nervous laughter, but Rick wouldn't let her go. Instead, grinning like the devil, he caught her other hand in his and made her help tug his slacks down over the sharp angles of his hips. Then he stepped out of them, and out of his scant briefs as well.

"Oh, my." Laurie gulped.

"Oh, my, what?" Rick teased, watching with brash, dark eyes as her gaze traveled over his body.

"Oh, my goodness! You . . . you are so beautiful."

"Glad you think so, 'cause what you see is what you get."

Their mingled laughter swept through the room like a tempest. In the midst of it, Rick lifted her in his arms and headed for the hide-a-bed. "Damn thing!" he cursed, hating to put her down, hating to let her go even for a second.

When it was open, the cushions strewn across the floor, they stood on opposite sides, seeming to pause for a moment. But the hesitation was only in Laurie's mind. Actually, everything happened very quickly.

With a keen laugh, Rick jumped into the middle of the bed and opened his arms. "Come on, darlin'. Cover me up!"

Laurie slipped neatly in beside him, but he was having none of that. In one swift move he lifted her on top of him, wrapping his arms and legs around her. She felt his flesh, his hair, the hardness and heat and power of him, all in that moment of contact. It was wonderful! She kissed him, rubbing her mouth across his, kissing his eyes and nose and chin. He kissed her back hungrily, tangling his fingers in her hair, nipping at the tender lobe of her ear. "Darlin' . . . oh, darlin', how I love you! Let me love you."

His hands met at the back of her bra and he snapped it open. Slowly, so slowly, he drew his hands around her ribs and gathered her breasts in his palms, his thumbs circling slowly over her nipples.

She drew a quick breath in through clenched teeth, the sound hissing like steam from a kettle on the boil. Never, never had she dreamt it would be like this. No one had told her, warned her. Maybe no one else knew! Maybe this was a special magic only Rick could perform!

Feeling the fever pitch of her excitement, he cocked one leg and rolled them both over so that he was on top, his body stretched along hers. Then, pushing himself straight up on his hands, so his chest was off her, he grinned down into her huge gray eyes. They were shot with gold and shining. But her hands still clutched her bra to her breasts.

With a sharp, wild laugh he leaped from the bed, found the silk scarf, and draped it over her. "Okay, darlin', so much for modesty!" And he pulled the bra away, and slipped her panties off, and lay down next to her.

She had turned her head to watch him, and he saw the way her lips were parted; her breath was coming quick and shallow, her eyes were glazed with rapture. Leaning on one elbow, he let his eyes roam over the curves of her body, taking in her naked beauty beneath the shimmering silk. And then, with a quiver of delight rocketing up his arm to his heart, he touched her, stroking with his hand along all the silken curves of her body, across all her secret places.

She moaned, crying his name, and he pulled the scarf away and covered her with his eager body, and she wrapped her legs around him, whispering soft love words against his hungry mouth. He made love to her then with a controlled and supple power, until his own body hit fever pitch and beyond and he exploded, taking her with him on a ride to the moon.

Later they pulled the covers up over their damp, exhausted bodies and nestled together. She lay with her head on his arm, and when she rolled onto her side, her nipples brushed his chest. "Ummmm." She sighed. "No wonder people spend so much time talking about this. It's quite wonderful!"

"Hmmmm, glad you think so," he whispered lovingly, dusting kisses across her face. "Maybe we'd better try it again, just to keep in practice."

Twelve

Pancakes . . . bacon . . . hot coffee . . .

The smells wafted from the tiny kitchen to Laurie, who was snuggled in the warmth of the tangled sheets.

"Mornin', my darling," Rick whispered, leaning over the curled body on the bed.

Laurie lazily opened one eye. "It's morning now, is it?" A contented smile curved her lips.

"Uh-huh." Rick's finger traced a path from her unclouded brow down to the tip of her nose. "But not for much longer, sweet thing; it's almost noon."

Laurie reached her bare arms up and circled his neck, drawing his face down to hers. "Come back here, then, Westin. Let me give you a good-morning kiss. And then soon I can give you an afternoon kiss, and an evening kiss, and—"

As his lips met and clung to hers, Rick felt his desire rise in him again like a flame, fierce and consuming. The smell of her, the taste of her mouth, the feel of her silken skin, drove him wild.

Reluctantly, Rick pulled away, and sat down beside her. He kissed the one bare shoulder that edged above the sheets and then smiled at her, his dark eyes engraving forever on his memory the way she looked at that moment—fresh and ripe and filled with the bloom of their lovemaking.

Behind the smile and the forced calm, Rick felt a twinge of fear as sharp and surprising as the delight he had felt the night before. Then, in the dappled moonlight, Laurie had given her love completely, matching his passion with her own. Now he feared the intrusion of the morning and its bright, uncompromising light. Would her fears and insecurities come tumbling back, an artificial judgment on their love?

"Why are you so still?" she murmured, opening one sleepy eye.

"Words don't matter right now, sweet thing. All that matters is you"—he kissed the top of her head—"and me"—his body slipped farther down, pulling with it the cotton sheets that covered her— "and the incredible love we've shared."

Slipping his hand beneath her shoulders, he pulled her toward him carefully, until the graceful curve of her naked body pressed against him. "Are you happy, Laurie?" he asked.

Laurie felt the pounding of his heart. "Rick, I . . ." She shyly met his eyes and felt her own sting with tears. "I don't exactly know what I should say. I feel so—"

Rick's dark gaze was intense. "What? Tell me. How *do* you feel, darlin'?"

Her slow smile was radiant. She placed one palm against his chest, her naked breasts trembling slightly with the gesture. "I feel . . . I feel *different*; I really do! As if there was a part of me locked away that I never even knew was there. And you found it! And allowed it to be free. I never imagined a sharing that could be so incredibly lovely." She nuzzled her head against the roughness of his unshaven cheek, then gently nibbled on his ear. "You've unleashed a wildness in me, Rick Westin; now what are you going to do about it?"

Rick's heart swelled. She was quite wonderful, his Laurie O'Neill. His fears vanished.

Running a hand along her cheek, he looked at her lovingly. "What am I going to do about it? Well, darlin', I'll show you what I'm going to do about it. . . ."

He released her only long enough to slip out of his jeans and tear his T-shirt over his head. Then he was back beside her on the rumpled bed, his lean body stretched along the sun-drenched sheet. "I'm going to nurture your wildness. Kindle it!" He pulled her close against his naked chest and ran his hands over the tightening swell of her breasts. "I'm going to savor it." He wriggled down and brushed his lips lightly over her nipples; the rapid beating of her heart was a gentle drumming love song in his ears.

"But Rick," Laurie said with a gasp, her voice a faint echo, "the bacon!"

His husky laugh tickled her belly as he dropped soft kisses along the smooth skin. "My darling, I'm going to capture your wildness and we're going to ride away on it, so far away you won't even smell the bacon!" He wound one leg around hers, capturing it lovingly. "I'm going to love you, Laurie O'Neill. . . ."

The next few weeks flew by in a blur for Laurie, a wonderful wild blend of living and loving. The new feelings Rick Westin had fueled totally consumed her. She couldn't get enough of him.

"Rick, it's crazy!" She wound her fingers

through his own, then pressed his hand to her heart. "Do you feel this? It's like this all day long, every time I think of you. I'm going to fall over dead in Senator Murphy's office if it doesn't slow down. 'IRISH LASS DIES IN SENATOR'S OFFICE OF LOVE OVERDOSE!' " She laughed softly into his shoulder as they walked slowly down a tree-shaded Georgetown street.

"Hey, darlin', I could write a song about it." He wrapped an arm around her shoulder, hugged her close, and began to hum loudly into the early-evening air.

"Don't you dare!" Laurie laughed breathlessly as she struggled to keep up with Rick's long strides. "People are already beginning to look at us!"

"Do you think they . . . *know?*" Rick whispered conspiratorially.

"I'm sure of it. How could they help it? I'm sure everyone knows! I can't keep this silly grin off my face, and I can't seem to sit still for longer than eight minutes at a time. Paula keeps looking at me with a strange smile I've never seen before, and nods a lot when I mention your name. And when I come in looking as if I haven't slept all night, she no longer asks me if I'm getting sick; she just winks!"

Rick laughed heartily as he guided her around the corner of M Street. "Well, my sweet, wanton thing, where do you want to eat?" He waved a hand at several restaurants fronting the bustling business section of Georgetown.

Laurie's smile wilted.

"What's the matter?" Rick lifted her chin with two fingers, his brows drawing together in puzzled concern.

Laurie shook her head briskly. "Nothing. Nothing." She forced a smile. "Anywhere you want to eat is fine."

"No, Laurie, tell me. Didn't you want to have dinner with me tonight?"

His anxious thoughts raced. They'd been together nearly every minute for the past three weeks. If he had a performance Laurie was there, sitting at the front table, her shining eyes leading him from song to song. He met her every day on the steps of her office building, and the evenings and weekends were spent laughing and talking, and loving each other into delicious oblivion.

He'd tried to be so gentle, so careful, so positive. He didn't want anything to shake her confidence or cause her a moment's doubt. But maybe he was rushing things a bit; maybe she was feeling too crowded, too overcome by emotion. Maybe she needed a little space.

He'd back off. He'd slow down. Damn! He'd do anything for her!

"Is that it, Laurie? Tell me!" Rick grasped her shoulders and turned her so that she faced him directly, her eyes gazing right into his own. "It's okay, darlin'—"

"Oh, Rick." Laurie's eyelashes swept across her flushed cheeks as she tried to avoid his gaze.

What would he think of her? What would he think if she told him his very presence swept her into such a tingling passion she could hardly keep her hands off him. She loved being with him, loved loving him! Loved the feel of his body, its beauty and secrets. She'd felt no regrets, no fears, nothing but pure, unadulterated joy! It was a world removed from reality, too wonderful to allow for recriminations, too thrilling to allow looking back . . . or ahead.

"Rick," she whispered in a voice so throaty and low that he had to bend his dark head closer, "I don't want dinner. I want to go to bed with you!"

Her face turned bright scarlet.

Rick bit his bottom lip to restrain the husky shout of laughter that swelled in his chest. He couldn't laugh; she was so damn serious! So wonderful . . . so incredibly special. Would he ever be able to anticipate Laurie O'Neill? To understand emotions so pure they nearly blinded him?

He shook his head slowly and kissed the top of her sweet-smelling hair, aware of both the lump in his throat and the painful tightening in his loins.

"Where to, sweet thing? Your place or mine?"

Thirteen

"Time to let the dog out," Rick murmured across the soft mound of pillow, his breath tickling her cheek.

"I don't have a dog," Laurie purred, feeling the delight of his nearness even as she woke.

Rick stirred, slid one arm around her lovely, naked back, and drew her closer. Tucking his knees behind hers, he molded her gently and naturally into the curve of his body. Then he raised one heavy eyelid and squinted at the bright light that poured in the curtainless windows. "What is that horrible noise, darlin'?"

The insistent, muffled ringing finally registered on Laurie's consciousness. She rolled over, burying her face in his shoulder. "Oh, it's the phone . . . darn. It must be buried somewhere under the cushions. Rick, don't you want to get it?" Then she heard what she had said, and shot straight up in bed. "No! No, don't you get it; *I'll* get it! Hold on, I'm coming."

She swung her feet over the side and pulled the

top blanket from the bed, wrapping it around her. But she lingered yet; sliding one hand back over his chest, she twisted her fingers teasingly in the dark thatch of curly hair. "It's morning, Banjo Man. How did it get to be morning so soon?"

"The phone, Laurie . . . ?"

A tiny, contented smile touched her lips as she stood and glanced back over her shoulder at that gorgeous body sprawled across her bed. "Don't go away, now."

With one final tug that released the blanket from where it was tucked into a corner, she wandered across the room and picked up the phone.

Rick propped himself up on one elbow. The memory of their most recent lovemaking stirred him, and he watched her lazily, fantasizing about the slender, responsive body hidden under that lump of blanket. He imagined his hands gathering her rose-tipped breasts, tracing the curve of her waist, stroking her lovely naked flanks. "Ummmm . . ." He flung off the sheet and walked buck naked across the room to her.

Stepping up close behind her, he slipped his hands beneath the cover and touched her skin.

She wriggled against him, holding the phone between chin and shoulder, reaching up to push her fingers through his sleep-tousled hair. The blanket slid unnoticed to her feet.

He kissed her lightly on the tip of her nose and she tipped her head to one side, talking into the receiver as she offered her neck instead.

"Katy, is this what you woke me up for? You're not talking sense. Of course I want to see you, and we'll make some plans and—What?" He felt her stiffen. "What do you mean, 'today'?" She gasped, spun, and pushed Rick away with a good, hard shove to the chest.

"*Holy Christopher!*" she shouted with the gusto of a seasoned sailor.

Rick shrugged and flopped back onto the bed, folding his arms behind his head. He grinned to himself, glad that her Irish temper wasn't aimed his way.

Laurie could barely control her voice, and she was gripping the phone as if to strangle it. "Katy, why didn't you say this in the first place? This is absolutely the most ridiculous thing you've ever done . . . and you've done your share! Don't you know Daddy will have the Pope out looking for you! And what about Mother? She must be sick with worry. And, young lady, you're not solving a solitary thing. Now, stop sniffling! Go sit in a corner of the bus station—and don't talk to any strangers! I'll be there in twenty minutes."

The slam of the phone was Rick's signal to wipe the grin off his face. "Something wrong, darlin'?"

Laurie was already tearing through the one closet in the room, pulling out jeans and a sweater. Her brows formed ridges above her flashing eyes as she tugged on her clothes.

"I can't believe she did that. I mean, can you believe it?" She shot Rick an exasperated glance but allowed no time for an answer.

"And there are two of them! Lordy! Can't you just see my father's face?" She ran her fingers quickly through her hair, grabbed her purse, and headed for the door. "Oh!" She spun around, remembering. "Rick . . . ?"

Rick had decided minutes before that he rather liked his place in the twilight zone; it seemed relatively safe. Now he rolled onto one lean hip and drawled seductively. "That's me. The guy in the bed . . . alone . . . lonely as hell."

Laurie melted inside. Lips in a pout, she looked down at him longingly. "Oh, I do wish I could join you, but"—she sighed—"instead I have a favor to ask. Two, actually."

One thick brow lifted slowly.

"May I please borrow the keys to your Jeep for an hour or so?"

"Sure." He reached over to the small table beside the sofa bed and tossed the heavy ring to her. "And the second, darlin'?"

Laurie nibbled on her bottom lip and started backing out the door. "Well, Rick, I, ah . . . Could you be out of here in thirty minutes . . . twenty-five, maybe?"

She threw him a wisp of a smile and disappeared. The door slammed behind her.

The phone was ringing wildly as she walked back into the apartment with the two teenagers in tow; she had known it would be.

Laurie threw her purse on the chair and glared at her younger sister. "It's him, you know. Your father!"

Katy O'Neill looked neither frightened nor surprised. She tossed her head, and her uncontrollable chestnut-red curls flew about her face. She was as lovely as her sister, but with a rebellious twinkle in her eyes that turned heads and caused parental ulcers.

"Laurie, Dad will believe anything you tell him; you know that. Nuns, even ex-nuns, don't lie. Tell him . . . tell him you *needed* me." She grinned over at her pixielike friend. "Right, Heather? I mean, we're not bad company."

When the phone finally stopped ringing, the silence that followed was anything but soothing.

Laurie stared at the two young girls. Her anger returned full force, having been softened only temporarily by the irresistible joy of seeing her younger sister. She'd always had a special affection for Katy, maybe because Katy always did exactly what she pleased, all the things Laurie would have given her eyeteeth to do, but could never quite pull off. Responsibility and other people's expectations always steered her right back onto the straight-and-narrow path, before her toes had ever felt the thrill of unorthodox soil.

This latest antic, though, was just plain stupid.

"You can't expect to stay here with me, girls. You're only eighteen! Good grief, you need to get back to college, to graduate, to—"

"From Holy Family College?" Katy groaned mournfully. "Laurie, do you have any idea what it's like out there? I mean, all the young nuns go to school there, too, and we have the *same rules*. It's worse than a—" She blushed, but stubbornly finished her sentence. "A convent! And I'm no nun."

Laurie sighed, torn between sympathy and annoyance. "It's your own fault, Katy. You could have gone somewhere else, if you'd just studied a little in high school. But you didn't, and Mom and Daddy thought this would be good for you, because . . . well, because you'd get more attention there. More—"

Her voice floundered to a stop. She did not want to be lecturing her sister, sounding like her parents or some prim Mother Superior. She knew Katy hated the small college, and honestly couldn't blame her. It was a good school, but not for someone with the rebellious spirit of Katy O'Neill. To Katy, it must feel like a prison.

She stood silently in the middle of the floor, the morning sunlight dappling her face.

"Hey, Laurie, your hair looks really nice!" Heather offered, her voice light as a bird's chirp. "I thought it would be, well, kind of jagged, you know, like you cut it with pinking shears."

Laurie's laughter broke the tension.

Like a kid let out of the principal's office, Katy flew across the room and hopped onto the unmade sofa bed. She glanced at the tangle of sheets. "You sure are a restless sleeper, sis! This bed looks like it went through quite a struggle. Heather, come on, let's be good houseguests and help Laurie straighten up."

Laurie felt her cheeks burn. Turning away, she hurried into the kitchen. Little did Katy know what had gone on in that bed! It was a delicious secret.

The only disappointment was having had to chase Rick Westin out of her bed at six o'clock in the morning. She had grown to love these mornings.

But this was no time to get all hot and bothered again!

Cooling her face in the refrigerator's chill interior, she pulled out a carton of eggs, butter, and milk. In minutes the eggs were scrambled and the smell of fresh coffee filled the room.

"First off, ladies," Laurie called into the other room, "we are going to eat breakfast. Then I'm going to call the office and say I'll be late. And *then*, I hope before Daddy calls again, we're going to figure out how to handle this mess!"

To everyone's incredulity, William O'Neill didn't call again, and Laurie soon left for work, promising the girls tickets to a fantastic banjo show that night if they behaved themselves and left the sights of Washington in one piece. And, she insisted, by the time she returned, she wanted a complete list of buses going back to Pittsburgh!

" 'Morning, Laurie," Paula greeted her as she staggered in the door shortly before noon with her arms full of reports.

"Oh, Paula, I'm so sorry I'm late, but you wouldn't believe how badly this day has started!"

Paula laughed at Laurie's distraught look. "So I hear! And how *is* your sister? I thought you'd take the day off to show her the sights. You've got time coming."

Laurie's mouth dropped open. "Now, how in heaven's name did you know my sister was in town? I didn't mention it when I called. The office grapevine amazes me!"

"Not the grapevine this time, I'm afraid; your father called the senator this morning."

"He what?" Laurie blanched, reaching out to the edge of the desk to steady herself.

"Yes, and he seemed mighty upset. Why, he scolded *me*, can you imagine? He seems to think you shouldn't have invited Katy here."

"Invited her?" Laurie's blood began to slow boil.

"Well, yes, that's what he said. And I can somewhat understand his point, dear. It's hard for young people to catch up on their studies. Maybe you could have waited until spring break; it's not far off."

Laurie's head was spinning. She could just hear her father explaining to Senator Murphy how faulty his older daughter tended to be in her judgment. Imagine, inviting Katy to take off for the big city. Another mistake made by dear, naive Laurie. But then, she was inexperienced, sweet child. Fragile, not intended for the big, bad world. Perhaps the senator could wisely advise her on this matter.

Bitter tears stung Laurie's eyes. This was more than she could handle.

She didn't even know whom to aim her anger at: her father, the senator for listening, or Katy and Heather for making up such a ridiculous story!

"Paula"—she ground out her words through

clenched teeth—"I think I'll take you up on your suggestion and spend a little time with my sister. I have a sneaking suspicion she might need close surveillance until I can get her on the first bus back to Pittsburgh! Here"—she dumped the papers on Paula's desk—"these are the reports the senator will be looking for."

Paula ignored the papers, her voice full of concern. "Laurie, you seem upset."

"Paula, what you see is not 'upset.' It's angry! I don't mean to take it out on you, but I could just scream. I'm not—no, I am *not*—going to let people push me around and manipulate my life. No, sir, no more. If my father calls again, tell him I'm meeting with the President and cannot be disturbed!"

The flurry of air from her exit sent the papers fluttering to the floor. "Oh, well," a very confused Paula murmured to the empty office as she took off her glasses and wiped them gently, "Mondays aren't terrific, even at the best of times."

Laurie walked for eight blocks before she cooled down. She stuffed her hands in the pockets of her tailored coat and explored the cracks in the sidewalk with great precision. At least *they* were relatively straight; you couldn't say that about anything else in her life right now!

And by the time she had circled the Washington Monument three times, she knew it wasn't just Katy and her father that had her mind and heart Indian-wrestling with each other. It was Rick. Her banjo man had woven such a romantic web around her that she had forgotten there was a real world out there: her parents, her family, her past, and her future. Oh, he had woven himself right into the very fabric of her being, and he was stuck there— right at the heart of her. Pull him out and something would surely break. But she had reality to deal with also.

She sighed, and then she noticed the little green spikes of grass poking their way up along the path, and the warm breeze lifting her hair. She realized suddenly that it wouldn't be long until spring arrived in full bloom—her first spring as Laurie O'Neill, *woman.*

The thought brought a soft glow to her face and helped soothe the churning inside her. Now if she could just get all the wrinkles ironed out of her life, it would certainly be a spring to remember.

Lifting her chin determinedly, she started to make some decisions. The first step was to get Heather and Katy on the bus to Pittsburgh. And then she'd deal with Rick Westin.

But, as had been the pattern of Laurie O'Neill's life lately, things didn't happen quite that simply.

Her apartment was empty, except for some junk dumped on the oak table. There was not a sign of the girls except for an open closet door that showed their hasty getaway—in two pairs of Laurie's new pants! She wandered into the kitchen and was absently grabbing for the refrigerator door when she spotted the note in Katy's left-handed scrawl.

> Dear Sis—
> A friend of yours called—the banjo player—and offered us lunch in George-town (imagine!) and a whirlwind tour! Said any sister of yours must be a terrific gal. I said, "Right on!" See you!
>   Katy and Heather
>
> P.S. The pants are a tad tight, but look great. Love ya.

Laurie's mouth tightened to a narrow, white-edged line. She stared at the note, at the refrigerator, out the tiny window at the grass moving in the soft spring breeze. How dare he whisk them off like that! This was *her* sister, *her* irate father, *her* problem! And she damn well wanted to handle it herself! Everything was getting out of hand.

The volatile combination of tiredness, worry, and confused, tangled emotions set off her Irish temper with the force of fireworks. But, short of calling in the CIA, there wasn't one thing she could do about it.

Laurie glanced at her wristwatch for the seventeenth time since seven o'clock. The deafening silence in her apartment was driving her crazy, and she still hadn't heard a single word from Rick or the girls. Obviously they had planned not only their day, but their evening, without her!

A spurt of good, old-fashioned anger brought a spot of color to each cheek. Well, she knew where to find them, and find them she would. Then they'd all see whom they were tangling with!

A cab was impossible to find, of course; traffic was horrendous, and the show was half over when she finally got to the theater. No one was out front at the ticket window, but she caught her first lucky break when Hans Hanson, Rick's producer, wandered into the lobby just as she rushed through the door.

"Laurie! Hey, glad to see you again!" He swept her up in his arms like a long-lost friend and kissed her lightly on the cheek. "Rick's been looking for you!"

"I bet! Has he got company tonight, two teenagers?"

"Your sister? That kid's a honey!"

"Oh, I'm going to wring that little honey's neck." She winked at Hans's look of surprise. "But I promise to wait until the show's over."

In seconds he had ushered her into the brightly lit room and straight down to the front table.

"Katy!" Laurie exclaimed between clenched teeth as she sat down. "You are in big trouble."

Katy and Heather grinned happily. "Oh, don't be mad. You said yourself we'd be coming to the show, and we're guests—of the star!"

"Hmmmph." Laurie did not want to be drawn into her sister's contagious excitement.

"Laurie," the younger girl continued breathlessly, "he's absolutely *wonderful*. If being convent-bred will bring me a man like that, I'll stay at Holy Family College for the next fifteen years!"

Laurie fought to hide her grin. "Katy, you are avoiding the subject. I thought Rick would drop you off at the apartment. I expected you to come pick me up, or at least call—"

"Oh, I know, I know," her sister whispered, "but Heather and I talked him out of it. I'll explain everything later. Don't worry about anything, Laurie. It'll all be fine."

She patted Laurie's hand with such blatant condescension that all of Laurie's pent-up feelings of anger and confusion swept back in one powerful gust. She glared at Katy's heavily mascaraed eyes and crimson cheeks. "Don't you tell me everything will be fine, little sister!"

"Sh-h-h," Heather and Kay said in unison as Rick came onto the stage. "He's back!"

Their adoring eyes swept up to the stage and fixed on the hypnotic black gaze of the man who had granted them one enchanted day and night. They stared at him like love-sick pups, but Rick only had eyes for Laurie.

He sang the rest of his songs for her. And when it was time for his closing number, he came and sat on the edge of the stage, lit by just one pearly spot. The light etched the planes and angles of his handsome face, and brought out blue highlights in his wild, dark hair. He smiled for her, and sang their song:

Come take my hand,
we'll fly away,
Into the sky, away from here . . .

Rick was at their table before the crowds had begun to leave their seats. He straddled a chair, leaned over, and kissed Laurie softly on the lips. "These two are great kids, Laurie. We've had a wonderful time!"

Trying tried not to react to his kiss, Laurie frowned. "Why didn't you call, Rick? Why didn't you bring the girls back? I've been a nervous wreck!"

Rick's eyes moved swiftly to Katy, who was coughing loudly into her napkin. "Katy O'Neill . . ." His tone was low, but his message was clear.

"Rick, I'm sorry." Katy's eyelashes swept dramatically down across her cheeks. "I know we promised to call before dinner, but"—she glanced quickly at Laurie, then back to Rick, "but we got a little busy . . . and besides, Laurie might have had other plans . . . like getting bus tickets, or whatever."

Laurie ignored Katy's stuttered excuses, her eyes still on Rick's face. "Rick, you *knew* I'd be worried. And the girls must go back. My father is furious! It's all a mess, and—"

Rick covered her hands and held them still on the polished wooden surface of the table. "Hush, Laurie. I'll explain it. Everything is taken care of."

The room was nearly empty now. The overhead lights had been turned off, and it was very quiet.

Laurie felt the pressure of his hands heat her body; the fire started at her wrists and blazed up her arms, until it pierced her heart. What it gave her was a delicious sense of release, as if she no longer needed to hold everything in check, no longer needed to be angry. Suddenly all she needed was him.

She leaned toward him, welcoming his body pressing against hers as an overwhelming tiredness hit her. "Oh, Rick, I don't know if I can take any explanations tonight. Maybe we'd better all talk it over rationally and calmly tomorrow."

"It'll have to be early tomorrow, Laurie," Katy cut in.

Laurie glanced warily at her sister. "Oh? And why is that?"

Katy's voice was soft, but her eyes sparkled happily. "Because Heather and I are leaving on the morning bus. For home. We need to be in class on Wednesday."

Laurie's eyes narrowed. "Just like that? Without a fight?" Her suspicious glance circled the table. This was too easy; something didn't make sense.

No one's eyes met hers. Rick was concentrating deeply on tracing tiny patterns on the back of her hands. Heather and Katy smiled sweetly into the darkening room.

"Well?" Laurie prompted.

"Yep. Just like that," Katy finally replied. "We have, ah, lots to do when we get back."

Laurie waited, knowing there was more coming.

"Yes," Heather gulped out. "Easter is just two weeks off, you know."

"Of course, Easter. How silly of me not to have thought of it." Laurie slipped to the edge of her chair. "What are you telling me, Katy O'Neill? What does going back home have to do with Easter?" she demanded.

Katy threw her arms up in the air. "All right, you might as well know. You'd find out anyway! The week of Easter is—"

"—exceptionally dull around here," Rick interrupted, his voice soft and cajoling. "I close the show just before the holidays; gives the crew a chance to get home to families, and all that." He shrugged, offered a grin. "And me, well, I just take care of a few loose ends around here. Begin oiling up my motorcycle—"

"See?" Katy's head was bobbing in agreement, the flaming waves of her hair tumbling around the sides of her face. "See, it was the perfect time, Laurie. *Perfect.*"

"For what?" Laurie's voice rose a decibel as the suspicion of what Katy was going to say next bloomed inside her.

"Well, the perfect time for Rick to come back home to give a concert, of course! It'll put Holy Family on the map!"

Fourteen

Numbness blocked out anger in the days that followed. Numbness and constant anxiety attacks.

"Laurie, I think you're letting this trip get all out of proportion," Ellen said as she flopped down on the sofa bed and bit into a piece of pepperoni pizza.

"You're right." Laurie took an avenging stab at her salad. "You're absolutely right! It's going to be even worse than I'm imagining!"

"Nonsense! You've changed, Laurie. Whether *you* see it or not, you're not the same Laurie O'Neill who let her father rule her life and emotions."

Laurie looked at her friend with fondness and picked her words carefully. "No, you're right about that, Ellen. I'm not the same; if I were, I would never have been able to leave the convent. I know that. But to have to face him for the first time, and with Rick right there . . . I don't know if I can do it."

Ellen tried to laugh away the doom in her friend's voice. "Well, I admit, the timing isn't terrific; leave it to Katy to stage a little drama! But it'll work out okay. Who could not be charmed by Rick Westin?"

"William O'Neill, that's who!" Laurie retorted, sending her pizza sailing across her plate. "Everything's against Rick: his offbeat charm and incredibly sexy smile, his profession, his gypsyish life-style, to say nothing of his motorcycle. Dad still thinks of motorcycles in terms of black leather jackets, stabbings, and gang wars!"

Laurie recaptured her pizza and took another bite. "You know, Ellen, the most incredible thing is that I'm sitting here worrying about problems grown women don't worry about. I mean, I'm twenty-three years old! What difference does it make what my father thinks? What—"

"It makes a lot of difference, Laurie," Ellen said softly, "because your family has always been so close and ruled so strictly by your father." She laughed lightly and brushed a stray hair off her forehead. "You know, as a kid, I used to envy you, because everyone in your family cared so much about one another. And your father, he was always involved, always so cautious about what you did, always so—"

"Stifling." A peculiar sadness crept into Laurie's voice. "And I can see from Katy that he's still the same. I know it's done out of love, and I do love him dearly, but it's not the way it should be."

"Maybe not. Maybe it's up to you to strike the balance. To keep the love and replace the other stuff with your own independent spirit. Once your dad sees the woman you've become, Laurie, he'll—"

"—send me back to the convent!" Laurie laughed.

"Seriously, Laurie, I think it'll be fine. There's only one thing that I see as a problem."

"Oh?" Laurie stood and began cleaning off the table.

"I don't think you've faced your own feelings about Rick Westin completely, about just how he fits into your life. And I think that's botching up your thinking about everything else." Ellen spread her fingers out in front of her and shook her head. "Just my uneducated opinion, mind you, but that's what I think."

"Well, stop thinking about it!" Laurie spun on her heel and stalked into the kitchen. She jerked open the refrigerator and pulled out a half-eaten pie. "It's not something that needs thought. It's *beyond* thought," she murmured to the pastry crust. "The fact that that man has me sweating at the mention of his name, standing at my window at night and imagining his hands on my body, feeling alive and full and wonderful when he wraps me in his arms . . . What kind of thought does that take?"

Ellen followed her into the tiny kitchen. "You're afraid, aren't you?"

"Me? Afraid?" Laurie laughed mockingly. "Afraid of falling for a guy, becoming dependent on him for my happiness, just at a time when I was finally beginning to stand on my own two feet? Afraid of falling in love? How can I be? I mean—" She shoveled a piece of pie into her mouth. "I mean, face it, Ellen, what do I know about love? I'm a two-month-old ex-nun!"

"Well, well, well!" William O'Neill's booming voice filled the small entry hall as the handsome gray-haired man scooped his shaking daughter into his arms. "My little Laurie has finally come home!"

Trying to breathe deeply against the smothering fabric of her father's shirt, Laurie willed her knees to hold up. This was awful! Why had she come like this, with Rick standing just behind her to witness everything that happened? She felt sick. Then a tiny voice screamed inside her head: You're not a little girl anymore, Laurie O'Neill! Shape up!

Pulling her head back until she could see into her father's deep gray eyes, she smiled brightly. "Hello, Daddy. I've missed you."

She slipped out of his grasp then and caught sight of her mother, waiting her turn, her hands wrapped nervously in the folds of the checked apron she never took off.

"Oh, Mom." Laurie hugged her warmly, breathing in the familiar odor of freshly baked bread mixed with the English Lavender soap her mother always kept beside the kitchen sink. Her mother's arms wrapped around her tightly and held her close.

Laurie held back her own tears and wiped a stray one from her mother's cheek. "Hey, this is a happy time—a reunion! Don't cry, Mom." She looked lovingly into her mother's eyes and stepped back.

It was when she stepped back that the hallway grew cool and quiet, almost as if a stranger had stepped into her stylish blue flats. Her father stood a few feet away, his severely appraising look moving slowly over her. Her mother stared at her, too, surprise filling her damp eyes.

The oddest feeling swept through Laurie: She thought for an instant that she should introduce herself to her mother and father. *Hello, I'm Laurie. Remember me? No, perhaps not. I've changed, as you see!*

But they *did* see, she noticed at once. And that was exactly the problem.

"Our Laurie." Her mother moved toward her first, her fingers touching the soft, gauzy blouse that lay loosely across Laurie's shoulders. It was bright blue, the color of peacock feathers, and was bound about her narrow waist with a colorful cummerbund that emphasized the fullness of her breasts. "You . . . you look wonderful, Laurie. Such a pretty blouse. It's—"

William O'Neill interrupted. "You're not the same, Laurie. You look different. What happened to the clothes your mother sent you?"

Laurie tipped her chin upward and faced her father with a brave smile. "I've bought my own, Daddy. But we have all day to talk about *me*. Now I want you to meet someone."

And, glancing over her shoulder, she met Rick's strong, relaxed smile. It amazed her how calm he was. He'd spent the whole long drive from Washington, D.C., laughing and telling jokes or strumming his banjo when she took a turn at the wheel. Occasionally he'd lean over and kiss her gently on the cheek, then point out a wonderful hill or twisting river he found especially intriguing. He had a way of making the smallest thing—a piece of old wood, a gnarled tree, or a bird's call—seem so very special. Laurie never tired of hearing his rich, deep voice wrap around her, winging her spirit off in some new direction. But all too soon the trip had ended, at the doorstep of the white frame house in which she'd grown up, surrounded by Irish love and protectiveness.

"Mom and Dad," Laurie announced, her voice louder than necessary, "this is Rick Westin, the man Katy has coerced into playing at the college."

For a brief moment that seemed an eternity, silence filled the hallway while William O'Neill's sharp gray eyes scrutinized Rick Westin with the precision of a drill sergeant. His gaze traveled over the wild, dark hair that fell onto Rick's forehead, the piercing brown eyes that never wavered, the tall, lean frame dressed in blue jeans, a sweat shirt, and rough, worn boots.

"Well, well, well," William O'Neill offered at last,

pumping Rick's hand, the expression on his face unreadable. "So you're the banjo player Katy picked up in D.C. And you seem to know our Laurie, here, too?"

"Oh, yes, sir. Very well." Rick smiled warmly and returned her father's handshake, ignoring the raised eyebrows and questioning look on the older man's face.

As formidable as William O'Neill was, there was one person in the family who never feared him, never hesitated to speak up when she thought the time was right: diminutive Frances O'Neill, whose rearing of the large O'Neill brood had given her a strength no man could match.

"Now, Bill, let the young folks come in and sit down. They've had themselves a long drive. You go along and run those errands I asked you to do." And she ushered Laurie and Rick away from the critical stare of the O'Neill patriarch and into the safety of her kitchen.

Katy soon rescued Rick and whisked him off to the college to test the sound system for the concert that night, and Laurie plunged into helping her mother lift the huge roast of lamb into the oven and crimp the edges on the berry pies. There was plenty to do and blessedly little time for talk. Seventeen relatives were expected for dinner later that day, seventeen O'Neills—and Rick Westin, her banjo man.

"No, Aunt Florence, you sit over there, near the window, so you can watch the birds." Frances smiled softly and helped the old lady to a seat near the head of the enormous oak table that filled the high-ceilinged dining room.

Laurie moved the salad bowl and squeezed a basket of rolls between the mashed potatoes and the string beans. She nodded at her elderly aunt and fled back to the heat of the kitchen. In there the table was set neatly and decoratively for the younger O'Neills: those cousins, nephews, and nieces who hadn't made it yet to the "main table," an honor that came with age and available space. The pies were cooling on the small back porch off the kitchen, and long-eared Rusty, the old setter, was curled beneath the bench beside the door, one eye opening and closing as each new person wandered through. Everything was exactly as it had been each Easter of Laurie O'Neill's growing-up years. Nothing had changed.

"There, now." Frances O'Neill walked back into her kitchen, wiping her hands on her apron. "Everything's nearly ready, Laurie. My goodness, dear, look at you." She reached over and tucked a strand of hair back behind Laurie's ear.

The gesture took Laurie by surprise. Her mother had brushed back her hair hundreds of times, maybe thousands. She remembered disliking it as a child, wanting to control her own hair, her own looks. She felt the same way now. Only now it wasn't her looks she was worried about; it was her life.

"Mom"—she looked hesitatingly at her mother— "having Father Flaherty come to dinner today—"

"—was your father's idea," Frances finished quickly. "He thought . . . well, perhaps it would be a nice chance for the two of you to talk. After dinner. Perhaps Father could give you some direction now, some help in planning your future."

"No, Mother!" Laurie's voice was clear and precise. "I'm doing my own planning now, sorting things out for myself."

She saw the hurt in her mother's eyes and immediately softened her words. "What I mean, Mom, is that I can't depend on anyone to make my decisions now. I have to do it myself. Everything's always been done for me, at home, in the convent; things were always mapped out *for* me. I never had to decide anything. Daddy was always there to do it for me, or Father Flaherty, or Mother Superior!" Tears began to press behind her lids, and Laurie fought valiantly to hold them back."Everyone meant well, but in the process, a part of Laurie O'Neill was left lying useless on the drawing-room floor."

"Laurie! How can you say such a thing?" Her mother stood straight and tall, her eyes flashing. "No one ever forced you to do anything you didn't want to do."

Slipping an arm around her mother's shoulders, Laurie kissed her gently on the cheek. "In a way you're absolutely right, Mom. It's taken me a couple of months to see that too. I mean, look at Katy! Dad's been suggesting things to her for years and look where it's gotten him! I *wasn't forced into* anything, but I've always wanted so to please others, especially you and Daddy!"

Frances nodded gently. She knew that was true. She had wondered all along whether her daughter would really be able to find happiness in the convent; Laurie had never seen enough of real life to prepare her for such a decision. And yet, at the time . . .

"And, Mom, I still want to please you two," Laurie went on, finding the rush of words strangely comforting. "But I need to find out what will please me too. What will make me grow into the fine woman I know both you and Daddy want me to be."

Frances O'Neill looked at her daughter for a long time. An almost overwhelming emotion pressed in on her. It was a feeling only a mother experiences fully, the incredibly poignant feeling of cutting the strings for the first time, letting a child go to seek her own happiness beyond the nest. In a painful moment of honesty, she realized she had never before had this feeling with Laurie. She had never before allowed her to go.

Offering her daughter an understanding, loving smile, she picked up a plate of spiced apples and walked back into the dining room.

At her entrance, the family gathered around the table.

Aunt Peg, as sprightly at seventy-five as Laurie ever hoped to be, wedged herself in between Rick and Laurie at the lace-covered table as the family began the festive meal.

"Well, young man," Aunt Peg demanded as soon as Father Flaherty had finished leading them in the blessing and while the room was still hushed from prayer, "tell me, did you meet our Laurie while she was still Sister Loretta Ann?"

Laurie groaned, Katy giggled, and a dozen pairs of eyes focused on Rick Westin, who was innocently chewing on a slice of lamb. He could only answer with the swift leap of one dark brow and a vigorous shake of his head.

Aunt Mary took advantage of his predicament to cluck her tongue and sweetly add, "It's a shame. She was a beautiful nun, you know. Seemed born to the habit." She cast a sad smile in Laurie's direction. "She looks different now, somehow."

Rick choked, then quickly recovered, fighting back his laughter. "Oh, yes, I have no doubt that's true!"

He shot a glance across Aunt Peg's ample bosom at Laurie's flushed face and added, "She's mighty beautiful now. And I can see where she gets it." He smiled warmly at Frances. "Those lovely high cheekbones seem to be a family trademark."

"Well, thank you, Rick," Frances replied graciously, a hint of amusement shining in her eyes.

Laurie's young man had gotten himself out of that one quite nicely, she thought with a peculiar satisfaction.

Jeremy, the youngest of Laurie's three younger brothers, who had finally made it to the grown-up table and was not about to let his presence go unnoticed, broke in. "Say, Rick, us kids were talkin', and we have a question . . ."

"Sure, buddy." Rick gave the youngster his full attention.

"We went to the cathedral to see Laurie when she wore a bride's dress and became a nun—"

Laurie covered her mouth with her napkin as a hush fell over the room.

"—and we were wondering if she can wear the same dress if she marries you, or if that's holy and if she has to divorce God first."

Basking in the warmth of everyone's undivided attention, Jeremy smiled and settled back in the chair to await Rick's answer.

Everyone quickly looked at his plate or the walls or the centerpiece of flowers in the middle of the table.

They need water, Laurie thought vaguely, panic blotting out all rational thought.

Rick settled back in his chair and looked around the table, then laughed so deeply and richly that even Uncle Henry, who didn't hear well and purposely never wore his hearing aid to family gatherings, smiled automatically.

"Well, Jeremy, those are mighty interesting questions you're asking. Mighty interesting. I'm just guessing at my answers, mind you, but I'm inclined to think the dress Laurie wears when she gets married is up to her. Whether or not that other dress is holy is a question we'll have to turn over to the reverend, here." He nodded cheerfully at Father Flaherty. "Next, I think that what happens between God and Laurie happens in her heart, and not in some court of law. And lastly, as to whether or not Laurie will marry me—"

Laurie's voice leaped from her throat. "That, brother dear, is nobody's business but mine at the moment." She drew a deep steadying breath, cast Rick a long, clear glance, and began to cut her lamb, her hand not trembling at all.

Glances were exchanged around the table. Katy winked broadly at her older sister. But it was Grandmother Jane O'Neill, her clear eyes sparking with merriment, who seemed to be enjoying the scene the most.

Laurie O'Neill was her granddaughter, all right, her favorite granddaughter. One could tell by the Irish spunk, yes, ma'am, that and the glint that sparked in her eyes every time she looked at her young man. Just like she, Jane, used to do with her Frank, God rest his soul. Well said, she thought, and lifted her voice. "Has anyone heard what the weather's going to be like this week?"

The dinner seemed to go on for hours. Everything looked delicious—but Laurie didn't taste a bite.

When Aunt Peg excused herself early to watch a re-run of *The Bells of St. Mary's*, Rick quietly slipped into the vacated chair. Beneath the draped tablecloth, the pressure of his leg against Laurie's gradually blocked out all other sensations.

In the middle of a particularly intense inquisition from Uncle Jerry as to what made young people shy away from commitment, Rick caught hold of Laurie's hand and twined his fingers with hers. Suddenly nothing else mattered.

Grandmother O'Neill grinned at the soft, sensual smile that awoke on Laurie's lips. Yes, sir, that Rick was just like her Frank.

"Folks"—Laurie's father pushed his chair away

from the table and fingered his wineglass—"Before we leave the table I'd like to propose a toast." He smiled gently at Laurie. "To my little Laurie, welcome home!"

Glasses were raised and words of welcome scattered like confetti as Laurie smiled in surprise.

"She's a fine young girl, our Laurie, no matter what."

Laurie's smile faded. "Dad, I—"

"No, wait, sweetie, I've got one more thing to say. It's a surprise, and I'm so proud of my little girl, I want to share it with everyone."

Laurie's face went blank. What could her father possibly have to surprise her with? A queasy, sickening fear swept through her.

"Laurie's been working for Senator Murphy for only a couple of months now, and already my girl has gotten herself a promotion!"

Laurie started to rise, trying to stem the flow of his words. "No, Dad, you're wrong—"

Bill O'Neill laughed jovially and reached over to touch her shoulder lightly. "That's my Laurie, always humble. No, my dear, I'm not wrong. Why, I spoke to the senator not more than three hours ago."

"No . . ."

"Yup, and he told me what a fine job you were doin', and that he wanted to take full advantage of someone so fine and honest and capable." He paused for effect, and Laurie slumped back into the chair as her father continued.

"It just so happens that the fine senator is up for reelection next year, and wants to open a campaign office right here in Pittsburgh. What's more, he wants our little Laurie to manage it for him— right here—*back where she belongs.*"

Laurie didn't feel the warmth of the smiles that approved her father's announcement, nor did she feel herself jerk Rick's restraining hand off her arm. She didn't feel herself rise. All she felt was an incredible anger tearing at her, peeling off layers of old habits, inhibitions, fears.

Slowly, she faced her father, her eyes wide, and flashing with a strength she didn't even know she had. "No, Dad."

"No? Of course you will, Laurie. I already told him you would."

"Well, I will take the responsibility of telling him I won't."

Her abrupt departure left no room for argument.

She climbed the stairs and flung herself on the bed that was still covered by the same frilly bedspread of her youth. She lay there, staring out the window at the familiar pattern of trees and houses, trying desperately to think.

And then she heard men's voices harsh with anger coming from the hall below.

Opening her door, she saw Rick at the bottom of the steps, her father one step above, blocking his way.

"You can't treat her that way, Mr. O'Neill," Rick insisted. "She's a grown woman—"

"And who are you, some rough-looking vagabond, to tell me what's good for my daughter?"

"I happen to love your daughter very much, Mr. O'Neill. And I know what she needs. She can't come back here now, don't you see? She's not Sister Loretta Ann anymore, not your little Laurie—"

"*Love her!* You don't even know her! She's not ready for the likes of you. Why, Laurie needs—"

Rick's voice was calm and deep. "I assure you, I can give her everything she needs. I can take care of her."

Laurie stormed out of the shadows and down the steps until she stood between the two men in her life. Struggling to keep her voice under control, she faced first one, then the other, her eyes flashing fire.

"Dad, I'm not coming back home. I love you, but your little Laurie is gone." Her eyes met his and held, braced by the courage that anger had lent her.

And then she spun on Rick, her composure crumpling. "And you, Rick—I thought *you* would understand!"

Before either man could reply, she rushed into the kitchen, kissed her mother a tearful good-bye, and drove off in the darkening night, alone in Rick's Jeep.

Fifteen

There was a sharp, angry rap on the door early the next morning.

Laurie had been expecting it, and she rose wearily, wiping her palms down the front of her robe. She opened the door.

"I've come for my keys." Rick stood with his legs apart, his hands shoved in his pockets, a scowl marring his handsome face.

"I know. I'll get them. Come on in."

She turned, not waiting to see if he followed her, and picked up the keys from the kitchen counter.

"Here." She held them out.

He took them, careful not to touch her hand.

"Thanks a lot for stranding me up there."

"I had to get away—"

"And me? You just left me up there with your impossible family!"

"No! Don't you ever, ever call them that! They're wonderful, loving people!"

"Yeah, you think so? Then how come you left, with no hugs and kisses for all those lovely people, no good-byes to Aunt Florence and Aunt Peg and Grandmom Jane? *And no good-bye to me!* As if I were on their side, one of the people making your life difficult."

"Well, you *are*, in a way! You're just like them, wanting to rule my life, decide everything for me."

"Me? I don't want to do any such thing!" He stared at her, wanting to take her in his arms and love her, but held at bay by her cold, hard anger. "Laurie, I want you to be what you want to be, live the way you want to live, and love me. Those three things are not mutually exclusive, darlin'! It's just that you equate love with dependence and—"

"And you don't, Mr. Westin?"

"No!"

"Ha!"

"What? What in the hell does that mean?"

"It means I think you want to be in charge, make the decisions, take over where my father left off." Angrily she brushed the tears off her cheeks, disgusted with herself for letting them fall. "I heard you: 'I can take care of her!' " she said, cruelly mimicking the words she had heard him say to her father.

"I meant, care for, as in . . . in . . ." Frustrated beyond words, Rick made an angry gesture with his hands. "As in taking care of some straight young sapling, offering it the sun and wind and sweet rain. That's all I meant."

Laurie stood silent, stubborn, her back half-turned to him. She was not going to listen, not going to be charmed out of her anger. She had to push them away, all of them, if she were going to get any freedom, any space to breathe. Even now she was strangling, as if a hand were at her throat.

She settled her face into a hard mask and shrugged. "That's what you say now because you know that's what I want to hear. But you were caught out yesterday. Then, when you didn't think I could hear, you said what you really mean!"

"Oh, you know that for a fact? Were you inside my head, inside my heart—or is this just something you know from your vast experience?"

"Don't mock me!" she yelled, wanting to hit him.

"Damn!" He turned, breathing fiercely through parted lips, his hands jammed hard against his hips. He shook his head, clenching his teeth so tightly the muscles popped along his jaw.

"Laurie, I haven't done anything. You're the one who walked out without talking to me. *You* left. You left me there, alone. You didn't even wait for the concert; you left me there with no one to sing to. And then I had to sit in the damn airport waiting for a six A.M. flight, and fly home alone. And *you're* the one who's mad? Hell, woman—"

"Don't curse at me, Rick!"

"I'll do whatever I damn well please. I am furious! Fit to be tied." A short, harsh bark of a laugh tore from his throat. "I can't believe I am even standing here—"

"Then don't."

He flinched, his narrowed eyes searching her face in disbelief.

She should have been still. She wanted to be still, to stop all of this. But it was as if her newborn anger had hold of her; she couldn't control it.

"Go, then." She jerked one shoulder up and down, her face empty. "Because if you're waiting for an apology, you're not going to get one. I am done apologizing for my life, my actions, my decisions. I'm done with it, hear me?"

"That's too bad, Laurie, because this was probably the one time you should have."

Rick strode to the door and yanked it open. He stopped with one foot in the hall, his hand still knotted around the doorknob. She could see his back heave with unspent emotion, and wanted to run and wrap her arms around him, hold him, love him, but something held her rooted to the floor.

When he spoke, his voice was rough, unfamiliar. "I love you, Laurie. More than I ever hoped to love anyone. And I know you love me, though you're fightin' against it so hard you're liable to tear us both apart. But, darlin', I leave Saturday for Kentucky . . . with or without you."

He turned, a rueful smile curving his lips, only his dark eyes betraying him. "Laurie, did I ever tell you I was scared of heights? Damn, the higher you go, the harder you fall."

An hour later she marched up the steps of the Rayburn Building and into Senator Murphy's offices.

" 'Morning, Laurie, how was your vacation?" Paula asked with a welcoming smile.

"Lousy!" she snapped, then softened her tone. "Sorry, Paula. Is the senator in?"

"Uh-huh, and alone. I'm glad I'm going to be out here, not in there." Ducking her head, she went quickly back to work.

Laurie knocked once on the door to the inner office, waited for the answering "Enter," and stepped inside.

Senator Murphy pushed his glasses up the bridge of his nose and smiled. "Oh, good, Laurie. Just who I wanted to see." He flicked the intercom button. "Paula, hold my calls." Then he turned his attention back to Laurie. "Now, dear, I spoke to your father and understand you may not want to accept that position in Pittsburgh."

"Senator, that's not quite correct. What he should have told you, what I made perfectly clear to him, is that I *definitely* won't accept that position in Pittsburgh. I do thank you, and I appreciate your confidence, but I find I'm going to be making some changes in my life and—"

"Now, Laurie, your dad and I have been friends a long time. I know he can be a little stubborn, a little opinionated—"

"Pigheaded, Senator?"

"Even that, dear, but he loves you."

"Of course. And I love him. And he will be proud of me, but on my terms from now on."

"Can I at least talk you into continuing your work here? You've done an outstanding job, and it would be hard to replace you."

"Senator, that's the nicest thing you could have said to me. Thank you. I'll finish out this week— longer if I'm still in town and you haven't found a replacement. But I am definitely leaving."

"And where are you going?"

"I don't know," she admitted with a smile, hoping her expression didn't show how much it scared her to say that. "I want to see some of the world, to see how other people live, so that I can decide how I want to live."

"But, child, with your background, how can you? How will you manage, how will you deal with everything?"

"That's just why I must. And, Senator, as you're so fond of saying, 'All you have to do is do it!' "

Paula looked up with raised brows as Laurie exited.

"How'd it go?"

"Great," she said, wide-eyed. "I quit."

"Want to talk?"

"No, Paula, I don't think so. I want to do this all on my own, and then I'll sink or swim with it. But thanks."

"Quite all right, Laurie. I understand."

* * *

Ellen was not quite as easy to keep at bay.

"What do you mean, you don't want to talk?" she shouted over the phone. "Of course you want to talk! I'll be right over."

Ten minutes later she was there, carrying a white paper sack.

"It's chocolate chocolate-chip. Ice cream helps me deal with stress. Have some."

"But I'm not stressed, Ellen," Laurie insisted, dropping onto the sofa.

"Hmmph." Ellen dismissed her words with a wave and a frown. "Could have fooled me; you look like death warmed over."

"I do not! I look fine."

"Hmmmph! And bad as you look, Rick looks worse. What have you done to that man?"

"Me? Did he tell you that?"

"Are you kidding? He wouldn't say a word if he were bleeding to death inside. Which is just what it looks like, if you want my professional opinion."

"I don't! If there is something I've had quite enough of, it's other people's opinions."

At the hurt look on Ellen's face, Laurie dropped her head into her hands with a groan.

"Oh, I'm sorry. But I just don't want to be made to feel guilty. I've got to finally start living my own life."

"So who's stopping you?"

"My father, my family, Rick—"

"Hold on a minute, Laurie Bridget Margaret O'Neill! Now, part of that I readily believe. Remember, I half grew up in your house. I know—and love—your dad, the beneficent tyrant! And all your well-meaning aunts . . . yes, they could try to live your life for you. Family has a way of doing that. I mean, look at me. 'Nun for a Day'! But Rick? No, you can't sell me *that* bill of goods!"

"You don't know anything about it."

"No? Remember, I've known him a long time. Seen him with a lot of women, some who wanted him, some who wanted to use him, some who just wanted to be seen on his arm. And that man has never been anything but honest and straightforward. Bold as brass sometimes, and not always easy, but always honest."

"I'm not talking about honesty."

"Yes, you are! Because if he said he loves you— which I'll stake my life he has, given the look of him now—then he meant it, Laurie! That means he loves you as you are, as you'll be forever. It's just too bad you don't know what a rare gift that is."

"Ellen—"

"Yes? Is there some other quality of Rick's you'd like to discuss? Bravery? Loyalty? Chastity . . . well, let's skip that one!"

"Ellen!" Laurie yelped, then she relaxed and smiled. "You did that on purpose, to make me laugh."

"Did it work?"

"I'm smiling. Will that do?"

"Not quite. You've got to see the foolishness of what you're doing with Rick. You're digging yourself into a hole, and for no reason. You want to love him; he's there. If you don't, if you're not ready, then tell him so. If you want to ride the hills with him, then go. If you don't, stay and find a job, or travel elsewhere. Do whatever it is you want to do. But don't hurt him *and* yourself; don't make yourself so miserable you push the whole world away. You know, that's taking the easy way out! Once again the decision is out of your hands. It's everyone else's fault: *their* bossiness, *their* stubbornness, *their* narrow point of view." She paused, looking Laurie square in the eye. "And you know better than I that none of that applies to Rick Westin."

Laurie sat for a moment, her hands folded in her lap. Then she sighed. "I guess I have a lot of thinking to do."

"Great!" Ellen said, leaping to her feet. "Then I'm taking my ice cream and going home. Now *I* need it!" And with a grin she squeezed Laurie's shoulder affectionately and left.

Laurie cleaned the apartment from top to bottom, then gathered a load of laundry and sat in the basement, watching the clothes spin in the dryer. Her thoughts were spinning even more frantically.

How should she know what to do? How should she know what was right? What was wrong? What to say yes to? When to say no?

Despite Ellen's words, she was afraid to let go of her anger for even a moment. It was like the little Dutch boy's finger in the dike; remove it and a whole flood of feelings would come pouring through to drown her. At least the anger was manageable; she could be calm, rational, do what she had to do.

And what she had to do was be a mature, independent woman. Right?

When she got back upstairs, the phone was ringing. She heard it from out in the hall and stood with the key in her hand, her forehead pressed against the door. Finally it stopped and she went in, dropped the clothes on the counter, and put up some hot water for tea.

She wished for a jugful of Raj's fiery brew, and then rubbed the heels of her palms into her eyes to banish the thought. Even that glimmer of a memory brought others sweeping into her brain: the party, Rick's fascinated, approving smile, the warmth of his arms, their lovemaking.

No, she mustn't think of that. . . of him. If she did, she was lost. She had to stay firm and resolute. She had to stand on her own two feet. Enjoy her independence.

Later that night the phone rang again. A tremor of excitement shattered her calm, and she sat for a moment with her mouth going dry, her palms damp. Then she lifted the receiver.

"Hello? Oh, Mom, hi. I'm glad it's you. Yes, I'm fine." She leaned one hip against the wall, her shoulders sagging, her heart slowing to a steadier beat. "And you and Dad? How are you both?"

Her mother's soft, warm voice droned on, and Laurie felt as though she had stepped outside herself, standing there talking and at the same time watching herself talk. She knew she looked quite calm and capable.

"No, Mom," she said in answer to her mother's final question. "I don't know what I'm going to do. Not yet. But I'll let you know. And don't worry, I'll be fine."

She hung up and straightened her narrow shoulders. There, that hadn't been so bad. See— she'd manage this independence just fine!

She measured off that miserable week by phone calls.

Tuesday night her sister called.

Her heart made its customary leap to her throat at the sound of the first ring, but it dropped back into her chest as soon as she recognized Katy's excited voice.

"That was some grand exit you made, sis! You'll have this dull bunch talking for years."

"Katy—that was not at all what I was trying to do! You know, I should really be furious with you, and I would be if I weren't working so hard at staying calm and in control."

"Sounds awful! But I'm sure there's some remedy. How's Rick been? *He* sure was not calm when he left Pittsburgh! I mean, the concert went great, but he was boiling!" Her young, audacious laughter filled Laurie's ear.

For a second she wanted to reach through the wire and strangle her little sister, or burst into tears! But she took a deep breath and replied, "I really don't know. We haven't seen each other this week."

"Are you crazy?" her sister screeched. "Listen, I'm coming back to Washington. *You do need me!* If you let them turn you against that wonderful man . . . well, that's just the most awful, awful thing I've ever heard! You can't, Laurie!"

"Calm down, Katy," Laurie said, her own voice wobbling with tears. "There's no need to be hysterical. I just have some decisions to make."

Katy didn't answer. She just slammed the phone down.

So much for Tuesday night! Laurie thought, the tears starting down her cheeks. She made herself a glass of warm milk and readied herself for another endless, empty night.

It was then, each night in the darkness, when she felt so hopeless, so lonely and unhappy, so torn apart that she wondered if she was growing and maturing, or just suffering.

Sleepless, she paced the room, filled with yearning for Rick, wanting nothing but the look of him, the feel of him, his nearness, his love. She placed her hand where his had been, on a coffee mug, a toothbrush in the bathroom, a certain book left open on the little table next to the bed. She saw him in the mirror, grinning over the top of her head as she brushed her hair in the morning. She felt his touch . . . the special way he had of reaching over and laying his thumb against her cheek, like a potter's mark, with such tenderness and love.

And she could not bear it. She had to love him, had to spend her life with him. And she cried silently for the emptiness her life had suddenly become.

Wednesday night Ellen called again, late, from the E.R. Laurie could barely talk, her throat was so raw from weeping.

"Damn, I knew you weren't sleeping. Laurie, when are you going to stop this foolishness? This stubbornness?"

"I'm not being stubborn, Ellen," she insisted. She wiped her face dry with the hem of her bathrobe, glad Ellen couldn't see her. "I'm trying to be sensible. Listen, I put it all down on paper, like those T-charts we used to make: pros on one side, cons on the other. Just listen to this list. Under 'Why not fall in love?'—need to be independent, need time, need space, need to think things through more clearly, obvious immaturity, inexperience, should travel, should look for a new job, should make other friends on my own.

"And here. Listen to this. On the 'Why fall in love?' side, you know what I have? Rick.

"That's all, just him," she whispered, starting to cry again.

"Isn't that enough?"

"No, it can't be." She groaned. "I mean, look, it's nine to one!"

"Yeah, but if the long shot comes in, you're really a winner! Hey, I'm just teasing. The point is, I think that if you want to fool around with that silly chart, there are lots of things to add on the side of love: happiness, delight in another human being, pleasure, sharing, caring, being happy to wake up in the morning, being glad to go to bed at night . . . in your lover's arms. Have I hit nine yet, or should I keep going?"

"You're probaby close enough, Ellen, and I understand what you're saying. But you've had the experience to say it. *You* didn't run off and fall in love with the first guy you met out of the convent!"

"Maybe you're just luckier than I, Laurie," Ellen answered flatly. "Now I have to get back to work, but I want you to think about something. Sometimes it's worth taking a gamble on the side of happiness."

So much for Wednesday! Laurie moaned, sniffing back her tears.

When the phone rang just before midnight on Thursday, Laurie was already bordering on exhaustion. Her head was pounding with the constant, futile effort of weighing and balancing all her conflicting emotions. She was tired right down to her toes.

She lifted the receiver and held it to her ear, her forehead propped against the palm of her other hand. "Hello?"

"Laurie, it's me. Rick."

She couldn't answer, but just sat biting her lips hard enough to bruise them, her whole body trembling.

"Laurie? Are you there?" She heard his voice deepen with concern. "Laurie, are you all right?"

"Yes," she whispered, "I think I'm okay."

There was silence for a moment, then his voice, softer now, edged with pain. "I'm kind of sorry to hear that. I was hoping you were as miserable as I am."

She felt the hot tears slide from the corners of her eyes.

"Laurie . . . it's Thursday, Friday morning almost." Silence, and then she heard him clear his throat, steady his voice, and she knew what this was costing him. "Laurie, have you made any decisions yet?"

She shook her head, spilling tears in all directions, and barely whispered, "No."

"Good! Then let me come over. We can talk it out. We can work it out together. We can—"

"No . . . No, I have to do it alone or it's no good, Rick. Somehow I've got to figure it out."

"Figure *what* out, Laurie? This is our lives you're talking about, not some math problem. Some crossword puzzle. Two down, happiness. Six across, pain. I mean . . . damn, either you love me as much as I love you or you don't! What the hell is there to figure out?"

"Me! Who I am. How I see the rest of my life! That's what I've got to figure out, Rick. I need more time!"

"I haven't got much more time, Laurie," he answered. "And if I did, if I said I'd wait another week, another year, would it make any difference? Or would it just prolong the agony?"

"Rick, I wish—"

"You know what *I* wish, Laurie?" He cut her off with the knife-sharp pain in his voice. "I wish I could make it as hard for you to leave me as it is for me to leave you."

She must have fallen asleep in the chair, because when she opened her eyes again it was morning. There was the soft patter of rain against her window, and daylight was filling the room with a pearl-gray glow.

Stretching slowly, Laurie pulled the chair over by the window and looked out. There were a lot of things to see: the lines and angles of roofs and house fronts, the long stripes of sidewalks, the rounded leafy shapes of trees. And people hurrying to and fro, alone or in pairs, wrapped in raincoats and hidden under umbrellas.

She was not going to work today, she decided. Instead she was going to sit here, watching the scene in her window . . . and she was going to take her life in her hands.

It sounded terribly melodramatic, and she laughed softly. Oh, that felt good; she hadn't laughed in so long, not all this week without Rick. Was that what her life would be like without him?

And suddenly, with a shock that made her sit bolt upright in her chair, she realized that was the one thing she had not thought of! What would her life be like without Rick?

Not just tomorrow, knowing he was leaving, knowing she'd never see him packed for the road, sleeping bag and banjo strapped across his back, helmet on, his lean, beautiful body leaning forward into the hills. She'd have no picture to carry in her head, no words of farewell, no leave-taking but this bitter ending, each alone. But it was not just tomorrow, which would pass.

It was not just the next day and the next, sliding into weeks. She could fill that time, with a job and friends, concerts and museums, a trip somewhere and visits home. But she'd never share those moments of wonder with him: nights camped out under the stars or sleeping on someone's feather mattress, listening to the old songs, the rich melody of voices and fiddles and a five-string banjo. But it was not just those endless weeks, which would pass.

It was not just the next year, her first as a

woman. She could get through that also, maybe, without him. But then who would laugh at her foolishness, share her joys, care about the way she grew and changed? Who would ever love her the way he did, dark eyes flashing, the connection so strong and alive between them, his every touch, his every smile encouraging, approving, nourishing her. Oh, God . . . he *did* love her! For her, he *was* the sun, and the wind and the sweet rain.

And even if she could survive a year without him, there'd be no reason to, because the rest of her life would be empty.

With a shout of pure joy, she leaped to her feet, then stood grinning at the empty room. *Okay, Laurie O'Neill, now that we know where we're going, let's get there!*

The first thing she did was try to call Rick. The line was busy, and she hung up and tried again immediately, over and over, until she was bathed in a light sheen of sweat. The thought of a good, hot shower and shampoo was like a drug, and drew her away for just a few moments. She came back, wrapped head to toe in towels, and grabbed the phone. This time there was no answer. She couldn't believe it!

She tried again all day and evening, at the town house, at the theater, but no Rick Westin was to be found. No one had seen him since his abrupt departure from the annual farewell party for the crew at the Stage.

It was love, and a sharp, pleasant anticipation, that kept her redialing his number. Never for a moment did she think he had left town already. No, if Rick Westin said he'd wait till Saturday, then he'd wait, even if it meant waiting in hell.

She cleaned the apartment, distributed the plants among her startled neighbors, and asked the woman next door to keep an eye on the place.

She raced out to shop, buying the few things her limited experience told her were necessities: a new pair of stone-washed jeans, already soft to the touch, a couple of T-shirts, a huge funky sweat shirt, some hiking boots, and thick woolen socks. A plastic poncho. A folding toothbrush.

It was all so easy, as natural as breathing.

The night grew late, and still she couldn't get hold of Rick. And there was no one else she wanted to call, no one she wanted to tell until she had told him. So she sat with her hand on the phone, and fell asleep in the chair again, and woke to the sunlight of a clear, shimmering morning.

This was the day! This was the true, shining start of her life!

She called a cab, then packed her things into a light, zippered nylon backpack, slipped into a pair of khaki slacks and a crisp oxford shirt, and tied the scarf Rick had given her around her neck. And then she locked the door behind her.

There was no one on the streets at six o'clock on a Saturday morning, and she delighted in having the city all to herself as she settled into the back seat of the cab and said good-bye to the now-familiar landmarks. She was at Rick's door in less than fifteen minutes, and knocked loudly, not caring if she waked the entire neighborhood.

But it was a stranger, a short, balding, round-faced man in a bathrobe, who opened the door.

"Oh," Laurie said with a gasp, jumping back. "I'm sorry I woke you. I'd like to see Rick Westin."

"Rick, well . . ." The man yawned. "Sorry. Rick moved out yesterday. I'm renting the place from him for the summer, and he was nice enough . . ." His words were stopped by another yawn, which he tried to hide behind his hand, while Laurie thought she would jump out of her skin. "Sorry. He was nice enough to let me settle in yesterday, so I'd be ready for my performance today. I'm a flautist. The flute, you know," he added, noting the totally uncomprehending look on Laurie's pale face.

"How nice," she said quickly. "But . . . do you know where he went?"

"I think he said he was going to stay overnight at a friend's, and then head out—"

Laurie was already running, the rest of his words unheard. "A friend's"! Who? Whom would he stay with? Hans? Raj? Ellen? Yes . . . Ellen's place, where she had first laid eyes on his dear, beloved face!

She raced down the street, looking for a cab as she ran. When the driver deposited her at Ellen's door, she clattered up the stairs and pounded on the door.

Dan answered. "Laurie! Hi, kid, long time no see." He grinned sleepily.

"Is Rick here, Dan? Please say yes!"

"Not anymore, it looks like," he answered, scanning the empty room, the empty couch, the one pillow and the blanket folded across the arm of the couch. "He must have left early. But Ellen'll know where to find him; she'll be home soon."

"I can't wait! He'll leave. He'll think I'm not going with him!" she cried, panic beginning to tighten around her heart.

"Are you?" Dan's brows rose in surprise. "Hey, good for you, kiddo! Ellen had just about given up hope."

Laurie hugged him, laughing softly. "Well, I'm not *quite* hopeless. I plan to make something out of myself yet! Listen, kiss Ellen for me. Tell her I'll call. I'm going to find Rick!"

And she was off.

As her feet touched the sidewalk, and the kindly cabbie waited for his next instructions, she paused. Where should she look next? Where would he be, her banjo man?

Suddenly she knew.

The driver traced their way back to her own front door.

There he was, parked at the curb in front of the building, looking up at her closed and darkened window.

He was sitting on his 'cycle, legs angled out from the machine, in jeans and a light denim jacket, his long, dark hair curling against his collar. Seen from behind like this, he did look a little wild and dangerous and unknown . . . and Laurie felt a tiny thrill of wildness climb up her spine.

And then he turned, without her calling his name or saying a word, as if his whole being sensed her presence. He turned and saw her as the cab pulled up, and he smiled, a smile that erased the pain from his dark gypsy eyes and made them flash with love and promise.

She felt the tears sting behind her lids as she slid wordlessly out of the car. What had she done to deserve such a loving smile, such a loving man?

He flung up one arm in salute. "Come on, my brave and wonderful darlin'. Come on! We're off!"

Laurie hopped on behind him. Wrapping her arms around his waist, she pressed her cheek against his back and whispered, "I love you, Rick. I love you, love you . . ."

"And I love you, Laurie O'Neill."

She felt the engine roar into life, and their journey together began.

THE EDITOR'S CORNER

Enthusiasm is one of the most powerful engines of success. When you do a thing, do it with your might. Put your whole soul into it. Stamp it with your own personality. Be active, be energetic, be enthusiastic and faithful, and you will accomplish your object. Nothing great was ever achieved without enthusiasm.   —Ralph Waldo Emerson

Enthusiasm is the fuel that drives the LOVESWEPT effort at Bantam Books. And our enthusiasm has never been higher for the love stories we publish than it is now in this bright new year. Our schedule for 1986 is glorious—combining the wonderful offerings of beloved favorite authors with those of exciting newcomers to romance writing. As you will see, we continue our LOVESWEPT tradition into 1986 of the marriage of something old, something new—but never something borrowed or blue!

STORM'S THUNDER, LOVESWEPT #127, by Marianne Shock is as exciting as its title suggests, while also giving us a rich, heartwarming exploration of what deep and everlasting love is all about. Patience Burke has been intrigued from afar by Storm Duchene for a very long time. When at last she meets him face-to-face, she is overwhelmed by her feelings for him—and it quickly becomes apparent that he finds her irresistible. But Storm is a man troubled by loss of a loved one and, even though he faces danger and death on the boat racing circuit, he cannot bear the thought of being bereft once more. And, so, he has decided never to love again. Yet how can he deny Patience? She may be younger and far less experienced than he, but she possesses a great deal of wisdom. She reaches out to him at just the right time and their relationship blossoms. Then, she must de-

(continued)

cide to pull away in an all-or-nothing gamble. You'll relish the warmth and wit of **STORM'S THUNDER**, and I'll bet that like me you'll be on the edge of your chair rooting for Patience as she makes her very risky, but necessary, move to win happiness with Storm.

Opening Kay Hooper's next romance for us, **REBEL WALTZ**, LOVESWEPT #128, is like stepping into a magnificent dream. Set in the South at an historic plantation house, **REBEL WALTZ** is the shimmering love story of Banner Clairmont, a gifted and beautiful young woman, who adores the mansion in which she's grown up, and dashing Rory Stewart, the sensitive and sexy man who fears he may have to take her beloved home away from her. Banner's shrewd grandfather believes at first that he is the moving force in the drama surrounding her and Rory. But very quickly he must acknowledge that it is Fate—whimsical yet certain Fate—that is working in its mysterious ways to draw this delightful couple together. Even as you close the book on **REBEL WALTZ**, its magic will linger, leaving you with the rosy glow and warmth of a lovely dream.

I think all of us true romantics believe that love knows no boundaries of age or position in society. And I also think you'll agree with me that no one could better explore that proposition in a delightful love story than our own Billie Green. In **MRS. GALLAGHER AND THE NE'ER DO WELL**, LOVESWEPT #129, Billie gives us two outwardly different people who have all the most important things in common. Helen Gallagher is a charming widow of some standing in her community; Tom Peters is a free-spirit, a bold vagabond who yearns to take her away from her small town and constricted way of life into a world of romance and adventure. Helen cannot resist the delightful rogue . . . nor can she turn aside the pressures to live out the roles of mother and citizen for which she's

(continued)

been reared. You'll thrill to Helen's discovery of her true self (with the best kind of help from Tom!) . . . as you keep your fingers crossed for her to find the courage to follow her heart. A truly unforgettable love story!

Several years ago I had the rewarding experience of reading several emotionally touching romances by Patt Bucheister, writing under a pen name. Now we're pleased that she has become a LOVESWEPT author— writing under her real name, of course—with **NIGHT AND DAY**, LOVESWEPT #130. Patt's hero, Cole Denver, is a perplexing man whose enigmatic personality just about drives heroine Chalis Quinn over the edge. By day he is curt, withdrawn, a sort of silent and distant macho man. By night he is charming, tender, almost a dream lover. What accounts for the changes in Cole? Why—when there is such caring and passion between them—doesn't he let Chalis into his life by day, as well as night? Getting the answers to those questions isn't half so difficult as knowing what to *do* with them! But Chalis is as spunky as she is sensitive and determines that with her help love will find a way. We hope you will enjoy this humorous and moving love story and give Patt a warm welcome.

Warm wishes,

Sincerely,

Carolyn Nichols

Carolyn Nichols
    Editor
LOVESWEPT
Bantam Books, Inc.
666 Fifth Avenue
New York, NY 10103

LOVESWEPT

Love Stories you'll never forget by authors you'll always remember

☐ 21603   **Heaven's Price** #1 Sandra Brown $1.95

☐ 21604   **Surrender** #2 Helen Mittermeyer $1.95

☐ 21600   **The Joining Stone** #3 Noelle Berry McCue $1.95

☐ 21601   **Silver Miracles** #4 Fayrene Preston $1.95

☐ 21605   **Matching Wits** #5 Carla Neggers $1.95

☐ 21606   **A Love for All Time** #6 Dorothy Garlock $1.95

Prices and availability subject to change without notice.

Buy them at your local bookstore or use this handy coupon for ordering:

Bantam Books, Inc., Dept. SW, 414 East Golf Road, Des Flalnes, Ill. 60016

Please send me the books I have checked above. I am enclosing $_____ (please add $1.50 to cover postage and handling). Send check or money order —no cash or C.O.D.'s please.

Mr/Mrs/Miss_____

Address_____

City_____ State/Zip_____

SW—1/86

Flease allow four to six weeks for delivery. This offer expires 7/86.